DOUBLE JEOPARDY

A RAIN CITY LEGAL THRILLER

STEPHEN PENNER

INKUBATOR
BOOKS

Published by Inkubator Books
www.inkubatorbooks.com

ISBN (eBook): 978-1-83756-388-3
ISBN (Paperback): 978-1-83756-389-0
ISBN (Hardback): 978-1-83756-390-6

1

The courtroom fell silent. Attorney Daniel Raine took a half-step toward the jury box. He clasped his hands earnestly and nodded solemnly.

"Justice." He let the word hang in the air. "That is your charge. To seek justice. To do justice. To speak justice."

Another pause, to let the words sink in.

"You have heard all of the evidence from the witnesses," he continued, "and when I sit down in a few short moments, you will have listened to all of the arguments of the lawyers. We will be done speaking, and it will be your turn to speak, first to each other and then to us. And the words you speak, whatever they may be, that will be justice in this case."

Raine gestured to the courtroom doors. "Out there, justice can mean a lot of different things to a lot of different people. In here"—he pointed to the floor between himself and the jurors— "justice is whatever you say it is. It's a huge responsibility. Take it very seriously. Please.

"Because the question put before you, the question you will answer with your verdict, is not what happened out there"—another gesture toward the outside world—"but what happened in here. The question you must answer is not whether my client committed the crime out there on the corner of First and Denny, but whether the State proved it in here on the corner of Third and James. Whether the prosecution put forward in this courtroom, over the course of this trial, enough evidence to overcome, beyond any and all reasonable doubt, the legal, constitutional, bedrock American principle that my client is presumed entirely and absolutely innocent."

Raine looked back at his client, the man's wide eyes glued to his lawyer.

Raine turned again to the jurors. "The presumption of innocence is not the last defense of the guilty," he told them. "It's the last refuge of the innocent."

Raine let his final words hang in the air. Then he nodded to his audience one last time. "Thank you."

He returned to his seat, the room still charged with the dying echoes of his advocacy.

The judge broke the spell. "That concludes the argument portion of the trial," he announced from the bench. "Now you will retire to the jury room to begin your deliberations. Your first duty will be to select a foreperson…"

Raine tuned out the rest of the judge's instructions. He'd heard them countless times before, and they didn't apply to him anyway. Instead, he gladly accepted his client's whispered praise for his closing argument and waited for the bailiff to call out, one last time, "All rise for the jury!" before leading them to their deliberations room. There would actually be one more time the bailiff bellowed that phrase: when everyone there reassembled to hear the verdict they had reached. It could be hours, or it could be days. In the meantime, he had other cases and other clients to occupy his working hours. And plans for after those hours.

"Keep your ringer on," Raine told his client. "When they reach a verdict, the bailiff will call me, and I'll call you. Until then, try not to think too much about it. We did our best. Now we just have to hope they do theirs."

His client nodded at the instructions, shook Raine's hand one more time, then departed the courtroom, still—for the time being, anyway—a free man.

Raine watched him exit, then turned his attention past the court staff and the prosecutor, all gathering up their things, to the defense attorney standing in the first row of the gallery. Sawyer Mount was Raine's plans for after work hours. At least that night. And more nights than not lately.

"Last refuge of the innocent." Sawyer nodded approvingly. "I might just steal that."

"Just give me credit," Raine replied, pushing his own material into his briefcase. He wanted to leave before the prosecutor so he could avoid an awkward walk to the door with his opponent. There was no good small talk to be had in that situation.

"Are you trying to put any other human beings in a cage this week?"

"No, are you trying to release any criminals back into society in exchange for money this week?"

"How long do you think they'll deliberate?" Sawyer asked as they entered the courthouse hallway.

Raine shrugged. "If they stay out more than a few hours, I'll count it as a victory."

Sawyer chuckled. "He's guilty, huh?"

"As sin," Raine answered.

"So, not the last refuge of the innocent after all," Sawyer observed.

"Definitely last defense of the guilty," Raine confirmed.

"How much is he looking at?" Sawyer asked. They had reached the main lobby.

"Two years," Raine answered. "It was just a car theft, but he has priors."

"Think he'll come back for the verdict?"

"I wouldn't," Raine said. "If they acquit him, the judge can't do anything about him failing to appear. If they convict him, why be there to get his bail revoked and get taken into custody?"

"Did you tell him that?"

"Of course not." Raine shook his head. "I'm not throwing my bar card away for some car thief."

"Did he pay you?"

Raine laughed slightly. "In full, up front. I'm not doing a case for free for some car thief either."

Sawyer nodded. "Yeah, I always make the thieves pay up front too."

They passed the security checkpoint and stepped out onto Third Avenue. It wasn't Seattle's prettiest street, or its cleanest, and it was especially bad around the courthouse. The first-floor windows had been boarded over with plywood, and the sidewalk across the street was covered with makeshift tents and passed-out addicts.

Sawyer pointed north toward her office. Raine's was to the south. "I'm going to go finish a few things up at the office. We still on for dinner tonight?"

"Six o'clock at Arturo's," Raine confirmed with a step toward his own office. "I wouldn't miss it for anything."

Almost anything, it turned out.

RAINE CHOSE to walk east up the hill to Fifth Avenue before turning south toward the International District and his office. It avoided both the urine-soaked park on Third and Jefferson and the tent encampment at Fourth and Yesler. Fifth and James was also where the King County Jail was located, the likely future residence of his latest client, unless the jury bought that "last refuge of the innocent" line. Raine really wanted to stop taking criminal cases, but they helped keep the lights on.

It was almost 4:30. The jury was unlikely to reach a verdict within the thirty minutes left in the day and would soon be sent home for the weekend. Raine just needed to drop off his briefcase and check his email before heading over to Arturo's. One nice thing about being a trial attorney, when the workday ended, you were already dressed for dinner at a fancy restaurant. If he got there early, he could even order a pre-funk drink while he waited. It was going to be a relaxing evening.

But not for everyone, apparently. While Raine's mind was filled with thoughts of dinner, drinks, and what might follow, there were other people in the world whose minds were filled with distress and anger. Loss. One such woman was standing across the street, in the cement plaza in front of the jail building. She was holding up a sign and screaming at any passersby who could hear her, whether they wanted to or not. Raine was definitely in the "not" category, but he was too close to ignore her. Not just because of the volume of her cries, but because of their content.

"They killed my boy!" she wailed. "And now they're trying to cover it up!"

No rhyming chant. No clever slogans. Closer inspection revealed she wasn't even holding a sign. It was a blown-up photograph of a young man—her son, presumably. Smiling. Handsome. With soft black curls and large eyes. He looked like his mother.

Raine didn't know the woman. He certainly didn't know her son. He didn't know what had happened to him, but he was sure there was another side to the story—there always was. The last place he wanted to be near was the county jail. He had a date, he needed to drop off his things, and his briefcase was heavy.

He crossed the street anyway.

"They murdered my boy!" the woman shouted.

Raine stepped onto the southwest corner of Fifth and James. The jail building was set back from the street, with a large, paved plaza between the corner and the front entrance. There was, perhaps, a small amount of aesthetic planning involved in creating a semi-welcoming space, complete with benches, in front of a facility no one wanted to be welcomed to, but the real reason behind the design, Raine knew, was security. Government buildings were prone to drawing protests; government buildings that kept human beings in cages even more so. Providing a plaza for potential protests reduced the likelihood any such protests would occur inside the facility. If things got really bad, the facility could be locked down and the threat neutralized from a safe distance. Forcibly, if necessary.

A small crowd had formed around the woman. Not more than a dozen people, but probably more than the woman had hoped for. And more than the jail was going to tolerate.

"What happened to your son?" Raine stepped to the front of the crowd. He was interested in the details. Though there was always another side to the story, the truth was often found in the first side. The defense, Raine knew well, could tailor their version of events after hearing the other side speak first.

"They killed him!" the woman shouted back.

Raine knew that already. Or rather, he knew she was claiming that. He also knew the strength of a claim lay in its details. "What happened?"

"They put him in a cell and left him to die," was the answer.

Not many details, Raine considered. He could have guessed the cell part. That was a standard part of being in jail. "How did he die?" he pressed.

"I don't know!" the woman wailed. "They won't tell me! That's how I know they're responsible!"

That rang true to Raine. Sometimes the details were in the lack of details.

"Okay! That's enough! Move along!" a deep male voice boomed from the entrance to the jail. "You are ordered to disperse! Comply, or you will be arrested!"

Raine turned to see a group of six police officers assembled in front of the entrance to the jail. They were dressed in black uniforms with no markings save the word "POLICE" emblazoned on their vests in large white letters.

The few other onlookers swiftly scattered.

"Maybe we should go." The woman wavered.

Raine thought so too. But not as much as he thought they should stay. "You have every right to be here. They killed your son. You're allowed to tell people that."

"You believe me?" the woman gasped.

Raine was starting to. The strength of a claim can also be measured by the response to it.

The police began marching toward them. Apparently the police felt the time for talking was over. But Raine was a lawyer. Lawyers never stopped talking.

He raised his hands toward the approaching officers. "I'm sure we can work this out. This woman is a grieving mother. She is simply trying to draw attention to her loss. Surely we can work this out peaceably, perhaps with some limited but reasonable restrictions on volume or location. No content restrictions, obviously. If I could just speak with your legal advisor, I—"

The lead officer, the tip of their spear formation, reached Raine and shoved him squarely in the chest with his baton. "Step away, sir. That's an order."

Raine struggled to control his reaction. He was larger than the officer, but he wasn't armed with a baton, let alone the Taser and firearm the cop also had on his gun belt. Raine wasn't going to win a physical altercation. Not one on one, and certainly not one on six.

One of the officers snatched the woman's sign—the photograph of her dead son—out of her hands.

"Fuck you, you pigs!" She grasped desperately for the stolen image.

"Ow!" the cop cried out. "The bitch scratched me!"

"This is your last warning!" the lead officer declared. "You both need to leave now, or you will be arrested. I won't say it again."

"Arrested for what?" Raine demanded again. "What crime is this woman committing?"

"It's my job to know the laws, sir, not yours," the officer responded.

"It's my job too, Officer," Raine returned. "I'm a lawyer."

Most people reacted negatively to that revelation, in

Raine's experience. Cops even more so than others. Raine looked again at the woman surrounded by a circling pack of policemen. The sadness Raine had seen in her eyes had been joined by fear and defiance. He turned back to the officer confronting him and gestured to the grieving mother. "In fact, I'm *her* lawyer."

That seemed to stun the officer for a moment. Or at least confuse him. But it failed to dissuade him. "Disorderly conduct," the officer answered Raine's previous demand. "Obstructing a law enforcement officer. Resisting arrest. Trespassing. And anything else I can think of between now and booking." Then he nodded to the other officers.

They threw her sign to the side and, in police vernacular, "escorted her to the ground."

Raine instinctively lunged to help her, but the lead officer stepped in between and pressed his baton against Raine's chest again. "Your client is under arrest, counselor," he growled. "One more move like that and you'll be joining her. Am I understood?"

The options raced through Raine's mind. Shoving the officer away and diving in to help the woman. Folly at best. Personal injury, criminal charges, and disbarment at worst. He fought his battles with words, not fists or batons. Not usually anyway. Not then, certainly. And if he really was going to represent the woman—something he was aching to do as he watched her being dragged away in handcuffs—she would need him to remain on the outside of the jail.

Raine set his jaw and jabbed a finger into the officer's Kevlar-covered chest. He could growl too. "I'll see you in court."

2

R aine was jerked to his feet, an awkward proposition given his arms handcuffed behind his back. He had an officer on either side and watched as two more performed the same maneuver unceremoniously on the protesting woman. She cried out in pain and fear as her arms were wrenched backward, but the officers paid her no mind. They marched her toward the jail, no doubt to book her on whatever charges they cooked up during the journey.

That begged the question in Raine's mind. "Am I being arrested?" he asked the officers. "Or simply restrained?"

There was a difference, he knew. The cops were supposed to know it too. "Arrested" meant he would be taken into the jail as well and booked on specific criminal charges. "Restrained" meant he was just being kept out of the way while they dealt with the protesting woman and would be released momentarily. He was really hoping for "restrained."

Unfortunately, there was a third option, which appeared

in the form of a patrol car that pulled up to the curb. It parked facing the wrong way on Fifth Avenue, north in the one-way street's southbound lanes. North, toward the main precinct for the Seattle Police Department.

"Ah." Raine nodded. "Detained."

The officers removed everything from Raine's pockets, then pushed him to the patrol car and stuffed him inside. They were nice enough to shove his head into his chest to avoid hitting it on the doorframe, but that was the total of their kindnesses. He slid awkwardly across the plastic seat, unable to stop himself with his hands behind his back.

The door slammed behind him, the cops threw his belongings on the front seat, and the driver pulled away.

"Are we going where I think we're going?" he asked the officer who was driving.

She didn't answer, but it didn't take long to confirm. The downtown precinct was only a few blocks from the jail. In a matter of minutes, the patrol car descended to the secure sallyport in the underground parking garage, and Raine was extracted from the car as unceremoniously as he'd been shoved into it. Two uniformed officers took custody of him and marched him wordlessly to the elevators inside.

"Nice place," Raine quipped. "Come here often?"

Neither officer replied. One stared stone faced at the elevator door, waiting for it to open. The other sneered at him and looked away again.

At least he got one reaction, Raine thought.

They took him up to the second floor and then down a long hallway until they reached a door marked with only the number 3. One of the officers unlocked the door while the other finally removed his handcuffs. Then they shoved him inside the room.

"Wait here," the cop ordered.

Raine was in no position to argue.

The door closed behind him, and Raine heard it lock. Inside was only a metal table and three chairs, all bolted to the floor. One chair facing the door, two on the other side. There were no windows, but there was a camera in an upper corner.

"Interrogation room," Raine muttered as he rubbed the soreness off his wrists.

There was no clock on the wall, an intentional decision to disorient suspects. They also had his phone still, so he couldn't be sure of the time, but he estimated Sawyer would be arriving at Arturo's in about thirty minutes. If they let him go soon, he could still make dinner. Surely they weren't planning on actually booking him on a crime. All he did was assert himself as someone's lawyer. Falsely assert, he supposed, and Making a False Statement to a Public Servant was a crime. A misdemeanor, but still a crime.

He frowned and began pacing the small room. Of course the only way they could prove it was false was to have the woman testify to that, and they could only make her testify if they chose not to prosecute her for anything. If they charged her, she had the right to remain silent, and they would have no evidence against him. They would have to choose whom they wanted to go after more. Her, for speaking out against them, or him, for standing up for her. And for being a lawyer.

He stopped pacing and frowned. He wasn't sure which one they would choose. They were probably trying to figure out how to go after both of them. Just because he knew the rules of evidence and how they would stymy a prosecution against him didn't mean they did. Maybe they were calling the DA's office to get advice. Maybe they were already talking to the woman about a deal if she agreed to testify against him. He couldn't make the same offer, of course. He didn't have any confidential information he could exchange for leniency, and even if he did, just his assertion of being her lawyer would probably be enough to make it privileged as far as the bar association was concerned. The Prisoner's Dilemma derailed by attorney professional ethics. Classic.

Raine looked again at the very not-opening door. He wondered how long it would be until someone, anyone came to check on him. What if he had a medical condition? What if he needed to use the bathroom? What if Sawyer only gave him fifteen minutes, then ordered takeout for one?

He dropped himself into one of the chairs.

He stood up again.

He walked the length of the room and back again.

He sat in a different chair.

He drummed his fingers on the table. Then his hands.

He got up and paced again.

He walked the perimeter of the room, running a finger along the wall from corner to corner to corner to corner.

He sat on the table.

He got up again.

He sat down again.

And still no one came.

He increasingly lost hope he would make it to dinner with Sawyer. He also increasingly needed to use the restroom. He was also hungry.

Cut off from the outside world. Anxious, hungry, tired, and in need of the bathroom. They were setting him up perfectly for an interrogation. But he knew it, so that would blunt their advantage. It wasn't like he would say anything anyway. If there was one thing lawyers knew, it was never talk to the cops.

He tipped his head back to stare at the ceiling.

But what he wouldn't have given to talk to a cop right then.

Finally, he heard the door unlock, and a uniformed officer opened the door.

"You can go," he informed Raine.

Raine was simultaneously relieved and irritated.

"That's it?" he complained. "I've been sitting in here for hours, and now you're just letting me go without even talking to me? Were you just messing with me because I stood up for that woman?"

The officer took a moment, then shrugged. "I don't know about any of that, sir. I was just told to escort you to the lobby." He held up a clear plastic bag with Raine's phone, wallet, and keys visible. "Here are your personal items."

Raine sighed, but then thought better of complaining about being released. He rushed forward and grabbed his belongings. "Do you know what time it is?" he asked even as he started reaching for his phone.

"Just after twenty hundred hours, sir," the officer answered as they both stepped fully into the hallway. Just after 8:00 p.m. He gestured down the corridor. "This way, sir."

There was no way Sawyer had waited two hours for him. He activated his phone and confirmed the series of texts from her, starting with inquiring where he was and when he might arrive, and ending with confirmation and a less terse than he had feared sign-off.

Hope you're enjoying whatever you're doing.

From someone else it might have been passive-aggressive. From Sawyer Mount, it was earnest. Too bad he didn't enjoy it at all.

He shoved his possessions into his pockets and returned the empty bag to the officer.

"I'm not leaving until I do one more thing," he declared. He glanced both ways down the hallway. "Where's the bathroom?"

3

Raine didn't like being messed with. Sawyer laughed when he explained it to her. He could see the humor in it too, but he wasn't amused. He hadn't been able to use his status and skills as a lawyer to stop the cops from ruining his plans. But he could use them to ruin theirs.

The United States Constitution, as interpreted and expanded over two centuries of legal decisions, mandated that a person, once arrested, had the right to have their arrest reviewed by a judge within twenty-four hours. On Sundays through Thursdays, that was accomplished easily enough. Everyone arrested the previous day was brought before a judge the next morning. The judge reviewed the police reports and determined whether there was "probable cause," that is, were sufficient facts alleged that, if true, would constitute a crime. It wasn't a determination of guilt or innocence, but it could feel like it because if the judge found probable cause, then the judge could set bail and hold the person in jail pending that eventual determination of guilt or innocence at trial, sometimes months later.

However, if a person were arrested on Friday or Saturday, special arrangements had to be made. A judge still had to review the one-sided police reports to determine whether, if what the cops wrote in their reports was true, a crime had been committed, but the King County Courthouse was closed on the weekends. So those hearings, perhaps ironically or perhaps just efficiently, were held Saturday and Sunday mornings in a windowless courtroom in the basement of the King County Jail.

The state of Washington had its own constitution, and the state constitution had a provision that required all court proceedings to be open to the public. That meant access to the windowless jail courtroom had to be open even though no one was going to spend their Saturday morning observing the probable cause jail calendar. No one except sometimes the family of the people arrested the night before.

Raine arrived promptly five minutes before the start of the calendar. He generally tried to avoid criminal cases, but he also generally failed at that, and so knew the schedule for most of the standing proceedings on the criminal dockets. He was dressed for court in a sharp suit and tie and had a new client file under his arm. The only thing missing on it was the name of his client.

"Which case are you here for, counselor?" the bailiff asked when she spotted him. She didn't know him by name —hence the generic "counselor"—but he was dressed the part of a lawyer.

Raine could only offer a grin. "I'll let you know when she gets here."

The bailiff frowned in confusion.

Raine took a seat in the front row to await the arrival of his client, whoever she was.

There were two other lawyers in the room. They were recognizable not only by their attire, but by their location and age. Both stood at the front of the courtroom, just below where the judge would sit, and both were young. They each lacked the seniority in their respective offices to avoid a Saturday morning docket.

Neither of them looked polished enough to step in front of a jury, but they were dressed well enough for the jail calendar. On the right was the prosecutor, a young man in a suitcoat and pants that went well enough together but were definitely not a matched suit. He was on the shorter side, with a thin frame and long hair he kept pushing out of his face as he examined the stack of files on the counter in front of him. On the left was the defense attorney, a young woman wearing a very similar not-quite-matched ensemble except with a skirt. Her hair was pulled back into an untidy ponytail.

The prosecutor would handle every single hearing on the docket that morning. The public defender would assist anyone who hadn't hired their own attorney, which, judging by the lack of anyone else in the gallery, meant everyone on the docket minus Raine's one client.

The way the hearings were supposed to go was simple. First, the prosecutor would present the judge with a written summary of the police reports, although not the actual reports themselves. These were still being finalized and approved. The judge would read the summary, then hear argument from both attorneys as to whether there were facts sufficient to support the filing of the charges. The prosecutor would argue there were sufficient facts; the defense attorney would argue there weren't. If the judge decided there weren't sufficient facts, then the person would be released. If the judge decided there were sufficient facts, then both attorneys would argue about whether the person should be held on bail pending a formal arraignment, with the prosecutor asking for bail and the defense attorney asking for release. It was a very important hearing, not least for the person who had been arrested, and called for careful consideration of all of the competing interests in the criminal justice system.

What actually happened is that the judge took the bench, and the three of them ground through the cases as quickly as possible. Unless the factual summary had accidentally been left blank by the officer, the judge found probable cause. The cops didn't put everything into it, just the information that supported their case.

The defense attorney never argued against probable cause, instead always saying, "We defer to the court." After the court found probable cause, the bail argument went much the same way. The prosecutor always asked for some amount of bail to hold the defendant over to Monday. The defense attorney always said, "We reserve argument on bail."

There were reasons for both positions the defense attorney took. Arguing against probable cause when the cherry-picked facts clearly established it burned credibility with the judge. Arguing and losing a bail argument could hamstring the next defense attorney, who would have to argue bail again at Monday's arraignment. But Raine knew part of the reason the cases were being handled so summarily was that no one wanted to be there, and the sooner they finished, the sooner everyone got to go home. Everyone but the defendants, that was.

The judge wasn't going to be happy with Raine when it was his turn.

After nearly thirty minutes, Raine was beginning to wonder when his turn might be. There had been a steady stream of miscreants and ne'er-do-wells who had crossed paths with Seattle's Finest the night before, but no sign yet of his mourning mother.

Eventually, the secure metal door to the holding cells opened to trade out defendants, and in walked the woman from the jail plaza. She was dressed in jail scrubs, and her hair was unkempt, but she didn't look too much worse for wear after a night in jail. She did appear a bit confused as she was ushered in by a guard and directed to stand next to some woman who was going to be her attorney for the next two or three minutes. At least, that was what everyone else in the courtroom thought. Raine let them continue to think that long enough for the prosecutor to call the case.

"The next matter," he announced, reading from his list without looking up, "is *The State of Washington versus Ophelia Wilson.*"

Raine rose to his feet. "I represent Ms. Wilson, Your Honor," he announced. "Daniel Raine, appearing on behalf of the defendant."

Everyone looked up at Raine as if shaken from a slumber, the slumber of repetition. Each had a different reaction to his announcement. The prosecutor seemed annoyed by the disruption to the flow of the morning. The defense attorney seemed relieved for the brief respite it would afford her. The judge seemed grateful for some change of pace. And Ophelia seemed surprised to see him again.

"Good morning, Mr. Raine," the judge said.

The name plate on the bench read "Judge Gerald

Higgins." He was a smaller man, with a bald head and wire-rimmed glasses. Raine couldn't recall ever having appeared in front of him before. He must have been relatively new to his position as well; judges also had seniority over each other. But Raine had provided his name, and the judge had been professional enough to use it. Raine returned the favor.

"Good morning, Judge Higgins. I was wondering whether I might have a moment to speak with my client before we proceed with her hearing."

Judge Higgins's smile faded.

Raine knew his request was going to slow things down. And the physical layout of the courtroom wasn't really set up for that. But he had his reasons why he wanted to speak with Ophelia Wilson before her hearing. The most important of which was to confirm she actually wanted him to be her lawyer. He'd asserted twice now that he was her lawyer—once to a cop and once to a judge. He should probably confirm it was even true before he went any further.

The judge was obviously not thrilled by the request, but he understood it. He looked at the guard near the door to the holding cells. "Is there a place back there where Mr. Raine could speak with his client?" he asked. He added, "Briefly?"

The guard frowned, but surrendered a begrudging nod. "I think so, Your Honor. There's a few empty cells they could use."

Raine didn't like the idea of walking voluntarily into a jail cell—he had narrowly avoided that fate the night before—but he wanted to speak with Ophelia before speaking for her.

The guard led them back to one of the empty cells, then left them there to fetch the next defendant on the list. A second guard stood outside their cell to make sure Ophelia didn't try to make a break for it, although she wouldn't have gotten past the locked gate at the end of the cement hallway they'd walked through to their makeshift conference room.

"Wow," Ophelia started the conversation. "I never thought I'd see you again. I can't believe you're really a lawyer. I thought you were just saying all that to bluff those cops."

Raine smiled. "Nope, I'm a real lawyer. And it looks like you're in real trouble."

"Then it's a good thing I have a lawyer." Ophelia laughed nervously.

"Well, that's what I wanted to talk to you about," Raine cautioned. "I'd very much like to represent you on this case, but—"

"You're going to help me sue the police?" Ophelia's eyes lit up.

Raine narrowed his eyes. "Sue the police?"

"For what they did to my son," Ophelia explained. "Wrongful death or whatever."

"You want to sue the government for what happened to your son?" Raine asked.

"I sure do," Ophelia confirmed, "and I'm going to need a good lawyer to do it." She took a moment to look him over. "You look like a good lawyer."

Raine appreciated the compliment. But there was another matter that was more pressing. "You realize you're being charged with a crime, right? Several crimes, I'm guessing. You need a lawyer for that first."

"I need a lawyer for that *too*," Ophelia corrected.

Raine leaned back and put a hand to his chin.

"Can you do both?" Ophelia asked him. "Are you one of

those lawyers who handles everything, or do you only do criminal defense?"

"Oh, I do a little bit of everything." Raine nodded. "Definitely not just criminal defense."

"Then I want to hire you to do both cases," Ophelia said.

Raine nodded again. He had to admit, he liked the idea. The best defense was a good offense. "Okay then, first things first."

"Get me out of here, right?" Ophelia guessed.

Raine offered a tight smile and a tilt of his head. "Almost. That's the second thing. The first thing is hiring me. I can do today's hearing pro bono. I saw what they did to you, and I couldn't do anything to stop it then, so I'm happy to help you get out of jail now. But if I'm really going to defend you against criminal charges and also sue the government for you, I can't do all of that for free."

"Of course not," Ophelia agreed. "I'll pay you from the money you get me for my son's wrongful death. What's that called? A contingency fee?"

Raine put that hand back to his chin. "We could do that for the civil suit against the government, yes. But we can't do that for the criminal case. It's against the professional rules for lawyers. No contingency fees on criminal cases. It's going to be cash. It's going to be up front. And it's not going to be cheap."

It was Ophelia's turn to lean back and strike a thoughtful pose. "I hear what you're saying. I've got resources. I can pay you. But I can't pay you from in here. Get me out of jail today, and I'll be at your office Monday morning with my checkbook."

Raine liked the sound of that. And he liked Ophelia Wilson.

"Deal." He extended his hand. She shook it gladly. Then Raine pounded on the cell door to let the guards know they were ready for their hearing.

Back inside the courtroom, Raine waited while they finished the case they were working on, then stepped forward when the prosecutor recalled, "*The State of Washington versus Ophelia Wilson.*"

The public defender stepped back to sit in the first row of the gallery. Raine stepped forward to take her spot at the bar, and Ophelia stepped into the courtroom to stand next to her new lawyer.

The prosecutor handed a set of documents to the bailiff to pass up to the judge. He provided Raine with a second set of the documents. They were the charging papers. The aforementioned Declaration for Determination of Probable Cause along with the Criminal Complaints. Raine reviewed them and couldn't help but shake his head. The scene he had witnessed the night before bore almost no resemblance to the charges and allegations being put forward that morning.

"The defendant is charged with six crimes, Your Honor," the prosecutor announced. "Disorderly conduct, obstruction of a law enforcement officer, resisting arrest, criminal trespass in the second degree, intimidation of a public servant, and assault in the third degree."

Raine stopped himself from making a quip about the obvious piling on of charges. They were being serious. He needed to be serious too. The disorderly conduct and trespassing charges were trivial. The obstruction and resisting arrest charges were a little more serious, but they were still misdemeanors. But intimidation of a public servant and assault in the third degree were both felonies. Ophelia was looking at prison time.

"Any argument as to probable cause?" Judge Higgins asked after reviewing the State's paperwork, just like he had asked for every case prior.

This time the answer was different. "Yes, Your Honor," Raine said. "We would ask the Court to find that there is not probable cause for the charges and release my client."

Higgins raised an eyebrow at Raine. "There seem to be facts sufficient, counsel."

"Maybe, if you only consider what they wrote," Raine replied, "but I can assure you, there's more to the story than what the officer included in that one-sided recitation."

"That's what the trial is for, Your Honor," the prosecutor interjected with a whine.

"I don't disagree with that," Raine allowed, "but don't hold my client in custody pending that trial."

Judge Higgins sighed. "I think we're getting ahead of ourselves, Mr. Raine. This is just a determination of probable cause. The standard is *prima facie* evidence, not proof beyond a reasonable doubt. I assume the truth of the State's evidence and decide if it would be enough to support the charge. That's all."

"That's a lot, Your Honor," Raine returned. "The officers stretch and mischaracterize what really happened. Ms. Wilson never intimidated any public servants. If anything, they intimidated her with their uniforms, weapons, and sheer numbers."

Higgins looked down at the declaration. "It says here she yelled profanities at them in an effort to influence their decision to arrest her."

"She yelled profanities at them because they took away the photograph of her dead son," Raine explained.

"And it says that she scratched one of the officers on the hand," the judge continued.

"Accidentally, Your Honor," Raine answered, "as she instinctively tried to grasp that photograph back from them."

"Your Honor, this is ridiculous," the prosecutor complained with a huff. "We aren't here to litigate the elements of the crime. The officers aren't even here to respond to counsel's unsupported assertions."

"Well, that's sort of the problem, isn't it?" Raine responded. "I would love to cross-examine the officers about what really happened last night, and I'm sure I will get the chance eventually, but I guess they're too busy or too important to bother being here today when my client's liberty is at stake. But that's okay. There's another way. There's another person who was there. Before the Court makes a decision as to whether there are really facts sufficient to support the charges, the Court should hear from Ms. Wilson herself."

"What?" the prosecutor cried out. "That's outrageous."

"You want to call your client as a witness?" Judge Higgins looked down incredulously at Raine. "What about her right to remain silent? Do you really want to expose her to cross-examination by the prosecutor this early in the proceedings?"

"No cross-examination by the prosecutor, Your Honor," Raine suggested. "I don't get to cross-examine the police officers. They aren't even here. Just let Ms. Wilson tell you that she didn't do what they say she did and then make a decision. She's here in person. I would argue the credibility of her live testimony should surpass that of a written report."

"I'm going to object, Your Honor." The prosecutor's voice cracked.

It was obvious he wasn't experienced enough yet to know how to deal with crazy arguments by old defense attorneys.

Unfortunately, Judge Higgins was.

"I appreciate your advocacy, Mr. Raine," Higgins offered with a smile, "but I'm going to decline your offer to have your client speak. I find that there are sufficient facts alleged to support probable cause for the filing of the charges. Let me hear your arguments regarding conditions of release."

The prosecutor beamed, as if he had won the argument himself. "The state is asking the Court to set bail in the amount of fifty thousand dollars. These are serious charges that strike straight at the heart of our system and the men and women who protect it. The defendant has shown a willingness to disregard the orders of police officers in her presence, so it seems highly unlikely that she will obey the orders of this Court to return for future hearings or refrain from similar conduct if released. Thank you."

The judge turned to Raine. "Defense?"

"The prosecutor makes a passionate argument," Raine began, "and one that could only be made by a young man who hasn't seen much of life outside of this windowless courtroom."

"Hey!" the prosecutor snapped.

It was a personal attack, but made for strategic reasons. Raine needed a quick moment to prepare for what he was about to tell the judge. He hadn't had time for a full consultation with his new client. But there were things a judge always wanted to know when deciding whether to let someone out pending trial: was she going to come back to court, and was she going to commit new crimes. The paperwork the prosecutor provided included a date of birth and a social security number. Raine could calculate his client's age and deduce her place of birth from the first three digits of her social security number. He took a guess about her criminal history.

"My client," Raine continued, "is a forty-six-year-old mother, with no criminal history, who has lived her entire life in the Seattle area. The only reason she is here this morning, and the only reason she was outside this building last night, is that her son recently died in police custody, right here inside this building."

Eyebrows rose on the bench and at the bar.

"That's not in the Declaration for Probable Cause, is it?" Raine pointed out. "The reason why Ms. Wilson was allegedly trespassing on public property, allegedly disturbing the peace of those responsible for her son's death. The reason she would curse at them when they yanked his photograph from her hands, stealing him away again. The reason she would desperately grasp for that memory of her dead child, allegedly intimidating and assaulting a squad of police officers dressed head-to-toe in riot gear."

Raine placed a hand on his client's shoulder. "Ophelia is not a threat to anyone except perhaps a threat to expose the truth of an overzealous police department eager to cover up whatever happened to her son. And she is not a risk to flee. She has retained me to represent her in this case, Your Honor, and any related cases that might be forthcoming."

A not-so-veiled threat of an impending civil lawsuit.

"She won't miss her day in court, Your Honor," Raine concluded. "She can't wait for it. She will be there, and so will I. Release her on her own personal recognizance so that she and I can prepare her cases to the fullest and ensure that justice prevails. Thank you."

Raine was pleased with his argument, and there was a silence that hung in the air to punctuate its effectiveness.

"May I respond, Your Honor?" the prosecutor asked after a moment.

"No," Judge Higgins answered without looking at him. "Mr. Raine has made several valid points, not just about conditions of release but about the entire nature of these proceedings. I do not believe Ms. Wilson is a threat to reoffend or a risk to flee. I will release her on her own recognizance."

"Thank you, Your Honor," Raine acknowledged over the prosecutor's huffing.

"Good luck on this one, Mr. Raine," Higgins added before moving on to the next case. "I'm curious to see how it plays out."

Raine was too.

4

R aine arrived at the office early on Monday morning. He was eager to see Ophelia Wilson again. Or rather, he was eager to find out if he would see her again. It was one thing to tell a lawyer you would hire him when you were sitting in a jail cell and he was your best chance at getting out. It was another to actually come down to his office two days later and pay him.

Raine would give her until noon, or when his jury came back with a verdict, whichever came first.

As it turned out, what came first was Ophelia Wilson, at nine o'clock sharp. She didn't bring her checkbook, because no one really used checks anymore, and she didn't have the kind of money she needed just sitting in her bank account. But she brought her wallet, and Raine accepted credit cards.

There were two fee agreements to sign, and two payments to be made. The criminal case was a flat fee, up front, "earned upon receipt"—the language the Bar Association allowed attorneys to use to mean "no refunds." The civil case was a contingency fee, so Raine's fee would be a percentage of whatever recovery he managed to get her. But there were "costs" that needed to be paid by the client along the way. Things like filing fees to start the case, court reporter fees for the depositions, expert witness fees for the trial.

Ophelia needed to put up a retainer for those costs as well. But she had good credit, or at least high credit limits. Both payments went through. Raine didn't concern himself with whether she could afford to pay them off. She was probably banking on him getting her a big payday from the civil suit. Which meant it was finally time to get the details.

"Let's start with the basics," Raine directed. "What was your son's name?"

"Tommy," Ophelia answered. Then added, formally, "Thomas Andrew Wilson."

"How old was Tommy?"

"Twenty-two," Ophelia answered. "He was my only child."

"Tell me what happened to Tommy," Raine instructed after the fee agreements were signed and his paralegal/receptionist/everything, Laura Johnston, left them alone in the office's small but adequate conference room. "Everything you know."

"Well, that's the problem," Ophelia answered. "I don't know very much. They won't tell me anything. I just know he's dead, and he died in the jail."

Raine nodded. "Let's start there, then, and work backwards. How did you find out he had died?"

"I got a call from the police," Ophelia answered. "I think it was the police, anyway. It might have been the jail. I think the man said he was a captain. But anyway, he said I needed to come down to the jail, and it was about Tommy. I thought they needed me to pick him up or post his bail. But when I got there, they took me inside. They'd never done that before when I'd picked him up—"

"So Tommy had been in jail before?" Raine interrupted.

Ophelia allowed a small chuckle. "Oh yeah. Tommy, he got himself into trouble a lot. Nothing serious ever, but he just couldn't stay out of trouble for long. He was a lot like his dad."

"What happened to his dad?" Raine wondered aloud before he could stop himself.

"Drug overdose," Ophelia answered with no apparent emotion. "When Tommy was three. Left me to raise him myself. I did the best I could, but he was always his father's son."

Raine knew what that meant. "So Tommy had a drug problem too?"

Ophelia nodded. The emotion was missing then. "He fought it. Really, he did. But that stuff is like a demon for some people. I thought he'd gotten clean again, but then they called me, and I knew he'd started using again."

"What was it?" Raine asked. "Heroin? Meth? Pills?"

"All of the above?" Ophelia managed to joke, probably to hide the pain. "I'm not sure what the latest was. He didn't talk to me about it. Only when I picked him up from jail or dropped him off at rehab."

"So that's what you thought you were doing?" Raine redirected the conversation. "Picking him up again and taking him to rehab?"

"Well, picking him up again anyway," Ophelia answered. "Rehab is expensive. I'm not paying for that unless he's ready to go again. It doesn't work if they aren't ready to go."

That had been Raine's professional observation as well.

"But then that wasn't it at all," Ophelia continued. "Like I said, instead of waiting out in the lobby, they took me back to the medical wing, or whatever they call it."

The infirmary, Raine knew, but he didn't interrupt.

"I thought maybe Tommy was sick, but..." Ophelia put her hand over her mouth at the memory. "But when I walked in, he was the only one in there, and a sheet was covering his face. And it was so cold."

Morgues are like that, Raine thought, again not voicing it.

"I was in shock," Ophelia went on. "I didn't start crying or screaming or anything. Everything just sort of stopped. My fingers and my lips and the tip of my nose, they all started tingling. And I just looked that guard straight in the eye, and I said, 'Who did this to my boy?' And he didn't deny it. He didn't say anything at all." She shook her head and looked down at her hands clasped on Raine's conference room table. "He didn't even say sorry."

"What happened next?" Raine prompted after a moment. He wasn't entirely unsympathetic to Ophelia's plight, but she had hired him to be her lawyer, not her therapist. He needed facts, not just feelings. "Did you formally identify the body? Was there a jail doctor present? Did you get their name?"

Ophelia shrugged. "Yes, I identified Tommy. There was a doctor there, but I don't remember his name. He had black hair, I think. And glasses."

That could be half the doctors in Seattle, Raine knew. But he could find out the doctor's identity from the jail records he was going to subpoena.

"They pulled the sheet back," Ophelia said, "and I told them it was Tommy."

"Did you see any injuries to his face?" Raine asked. The

police might have escorted Tommy to the ground before booking him too.

But Ophelia shook her head. "No. No, he looked fine. Pale, but fine. Like he was sleeping. Like all those times he was growing up when he was sick and I watched him sleep. All those times I was there for him. But I wasn't there for him this time. I wasn't there for him!"

The dam broke, and Ophelia Wilson finally let herself sob at the death of her only child. Right there in Raine's conference room.

After an uncomfortable moment, Raine stood up and leaned into the hallway to call to his assistant, "Laura? Could we get some tissues in here?"

Raine returned to his seat next to his crying client and offered a, "There, there," and an awkward pat on her shoulder.

"Did they tell you anything else?" he asked, trying to get her back on track. The tears were understandable, but he wanted her to save some for the jury. "What happened? How he died? Anything?"

Ophelia shook her head and looked up to accept the box of tissues Laura had quickly brought. She wiped her nose and shook her head again. "No. Nothing. They wouldn't tell me anything. That's how I know they were covering something up. If he had fallen and hit his head, they would have told me that, right? Or if another inmate stabbed him or something, why not tell me that? No, it was something they did. I know it. They wouldn't even tell me what he was in for. How is that a secret?"

"It's not," Raine answered. "It will be in the autopsy report. I'll get a copy of that. They may not give it to you, but they'll have to give it to your lawyer. When did this happen?" A question he probably should have asked sooner.

"Last Wednesday," Ophelia answered. She blew her nose and wiped the drying tears from the corners of her eyes. "I spent all day Thursday trying to get answers, but no one would even talk to me. That's why I went out there on Friday."

"Wednesday," Raine repeated, more to himself than his client. That was cutting it close, but there was a chance. He stood up. "Thank you, Ophelia. I will get the lawsuit filed right away. But we need to end our meeting. I need to go before it's too late."

"Go? Where? Before what's too late?"

"The medical examiner's office," Raine answered. "Before they destroy the evidence."

5

The King County Medical Examiner's Office was located in the King County Administrative Building at Fourth Avenue and James Street. It was directly between the King County Courthouse on Third Avenue and the King County Jail on Fifth Avenue. The secure skybridge to transport inmates from the jail to the courthouse actually rested atop the roof of the Admin Building.

Raine had unknowingly walked past Tommy Wilson's remains on his way to meet Tommy's mother for the first time that previous Friday. He could only hope those remains were still there.

Raine had been to the ME's Office before, but he wasn't what one might consider a regular. He wasn't a homicide detective or career violent crimes prosecutor. But he was in a suit, and the only people left in Seattle who wore suits were lawyers. So the receptionist, while she might not have known who he was, she knew what he was.

"Morning, counselor," she greeted him. "How can I help you?"

"Good morning," Raine returned the greeting. "My name is Daniel Raine, and I'm—"

His introduction was cut short by the ring of his phone. He tried to ignore it, but it rang again. "I'm sorry." He raised a finger to the receptionist. "This will just take a moment."

He pulled his phone out of his pocket and looked at the incoming number. He didn't recognize it at first. The area code was 206, but that was everyone in Seattle. The next three, 403, were familiar somehow, but he didn't recognize the last four. He stared at the number for a moment longer, eager to get back to his business at hand, when he suddenly recognized the 403. That was the prefix for the court. It was the bailiff from his trial.

"Raine," he answered the phone, heart thumping.

"The jury has a verdict," the bailiff said. "The judge is ordering everyone to assemble in her courtroom in thirty minutes. Have your client appear with you."

Raine acknowledged the information and promised he would contact his client. Or try at least. He hung up and looked at the receptionist again. Thirty minutes wasn't enough time.

"Is everything all right?" she asked.

Raine frowned. "I don't suppose the medical examiner who did the Wilson autopsy is here right now?"

"Wilson?" The receptionist frowned. "I don't know all of the names. Do you know when it was conducted? And, of course, how are you related to the case?"

That wasn't going to help, Raine knew. He took a moment to think, but he was already down to twenty-eight minutes before he needed to be in court. "Can you just ask them not to dispose of any bodies until I get back?"

The receptionist cocked her head. "That's kind of all we do here. When will you be back?"

Raine considered. "It depends on the verdict."

"What?"

"Never mind."

Raine couldn't take any more time to argue with the receptionist. He gave her Tommy's full name and estimated that the autopsy took place sometime between Wednesday and that morning. He told her he was a lawyer, but he didn't tell her for whom. He just implored her not to let the body be destroyed while he attended to one of his other clients.

She reacted in a way that gave him no confidence at all that she would do anything to comply with his request.

Raine hurried to the elevator bank, only to wait for the elevator to arrive. He hurried outside, only to wait for the pedestrian signal to change to "WALK." He hurried into the courthouse, only to wait his turn to pass through the metal detectors. And he called his client, only to wait to leave him a voicemail.

"The jury has a verdict," he informed the recording. "You need to be in the courtroom in fifteen minutes."

In reality, there were seventeen minutes still. But then Raine had to wait for the elevator up to the proper floor.

By the time he got inside the courtroom, there were only twelve minutes left. The prosecutor was already there; her office was in the courthouse, one floor down. The bailiff and the court reporter were too. All they had left to do was wait for the judge. And Raine's client.

Eleven minutes later the judge came out. A minute after that, Raine's client still wasn't there.

"Where is your client, Mr. Raine?" the judge demanded.

"I called him, Your Honor," Raine explained, "but he didn't answer. I left him a voicemail."

The judge frowned. "How long do you expect us to wait?"

Raine considered the options. And the receptionist at the Medical Examiner's Office. "I think we can proceed without him, Your Honor."

"Without him?" the prosecutor fairly screeched. "What if it's a guilty verdict? I'm going to ask that he be remanded into custody."

"What if it's a not-guilty verdict?" Raine countered. "Then he's free to leave with or without the State's or the Court's permission. He doesn't need to be here for an acquittal. I'm happy to stand in for him."

The judge raised an eyebrow at him. "You're that confident, are you?"

I'm that busy, Raine thought, but he couldn't say that. "I don't want to waste the Court's time. And I especially don't want to waste the jury's time. I have no idea how long it will take to get a hold of my client. I told him to keep his ringer on, but if he listened to people and followed good advice, he wouldn't be in the position he is now, would he?"

"I would very much prefer to wait for the defendant to be present for the verdict, Your Honor," the prosecutor put in.

"I mean, we could wait, I suppose," Raine offered. "But while we sit out here waiting for my phone to ring, the jurors will just be sitting back there, wondering what's going on. They will probably start talking about the case again. One of them might even change their mind. Then we wouldn't have a verdict anymore. We might even end up with a hung jury. But I guess that's good for me—beats a conviction."

The prosecutor's eyes widened at the mention of a hung

jury. A hung jury meant a mistrial. A mistrial meant having to do the trial all over again. And a second trial never went as well for the prosecution.

"Never mind, Your Honor," the prosecutor said. "The State is ready to take the verdict. Defense counsel is correct. If it's an acquittal, it doesn't matter that he's not here. If it's a conviction, we can issue a warrant for his arrest."

"Seems fair to me," Raine agreed.

The judge frowned, and deeply. He looked at the clock on the courtroom wall. "It's still early in the day," he observed. "The trial took a long time. I'm not going to rush the taking of the verdict. We can wait at least a little bit longer."

Raine suppressed a sigh.

"Call your client again, Mr. Raine," the judge directed. "Call him every five minutes if you have to, but get a hold of him and tell him to get to this courtroom as soon as he possibly can."

"Yes, Your Honor," Raine had to agree. "How long are we going to wait?"

"As long as it takes," the judge answered. "As long as it takes."

Raine nodded. He was afraid of that.

RAINE SPENT the next hour calling his client, leaving seven more voicemails in the process, each more insistent than the last. By the end of that hour, Raine knew his client wasn't coming back to court. Raine had given a great closing argument, but it hadn't convinced even his client. Better to be out, on a warrant, than in, awaiting sentencing.

"Did you get a hold of him?" the prosecutor whined when Raine returned to the courtroom after the final voicemail.

"No," he admitted. "And I don't think I'm going to. You might want to get that warrant paperwork ready."

"What do you think I've been doing while you were trying to reach him?" The prosecutor grinned and held up the papers for the judge to sign. "I'm ready if you are."

Raine shrugged. He was as ready as he was going to be. He informed the bailiff of as much and took his seat at the defense table.

The judge didn't come out. Everyone sat there for another thirty minutes.

The bailiff's telephone rang. He picked it up, held a brief and whispered conversation, then hung up and looked at Raine. "The judge says to try one more time. Then he'll come out."

Raine shrugged and pulled out his phone. He dialed the number. The call went to voicemail. He hung up. "No dice. Let's get this over with."

The bailiff picked up his phone, had another and briefer whispered conversation, and a few moments later the judge took the bench.

"All rise!" the bailiff called out. "The King County Superior Court is back in session!"

"Please be seated," the judge instructed. "You were unable to reach your client, Mr. Raine?"

"I'm afraid so, Your Honor," Raine answered. "I suggest we proceed without him."

"I concur," the prosecutor added.

The judge sighed, but then nodded to his bailiff. "Bring out the jury."

Raine and the prosecutor both stood for the entrance of the jurors. They marched from the jury room into the jury box. One of them held the verdict form. All of them looked confused when they saw Raine standing alone at the defense table.

"Ladies and gentlemen of the jury, good morning," the judge greeted them.

Raine stole a glance at the clock to confirm it was still morning. It was, but only just barely. In twelve more minutes it would be noon.

"The bailiff has informed me that the jury has reached a verdict."

The foreperson, the one holding the verdict form, stood up. "Yes, Your Honor, we have."

The judge nodded and paused before saying anything more. His mouth twisted into a conflicted knot; then he let out a long breath. "The defendant," he told the jurors, "has exercised his constitutional right not to be present at the reading of the verdict."

That, Raine knew, was a load of malarky. There was no such constitutional right. But it was better than telling the jurors that he had failed to appear. Until the verdict was read and accepted, there was a chance of something happening and the jury needing to continue their deliberations. Maybe they misunderstood the judge's instructions and thought a simple majority was enough to convict. If the verdict form said "Guilty, by a vote of 7 to 5," then the judge would send them back. But that would be impossible if they were tainted with the knowledge that the defendant was certain enough in his own guilt not to be there when the jury pronounced it.

The judge's explanation seemed to assuage the jurors'

concerns, and the foreperson handed the verdict form to the bailiff before sitting down again.

The bailiff walked the form over to the judge.

The judge read it to himself, then looked up. Normally, he might have ordered, "The defendant will rise for the reading of the verdict." But instead he looked back down again and announced the jury's decision. "We, the jury, in the above-captioned case, do hereby find the defendant..."

Even without his client there, Raine's heart was beating faster than normal. If he ever stopped being nervous about a verdict, it would be time to retire.

"...*not guilty* of the crime of Theft of a Motor Vehicle."

Raine smiled and nodded. He looked to the jurors and mouthed, "Thank you." His client would like the next voicemail.

The prosecutor threw his warrant paperwork down on his table and did a terrible job of not pouting like a child. Prosecutors were too used to winning to know how to lose graciously. Most of them anyway. That just made an acquittal all the more satisfying.

The judge formally thanked the jurors for their service and gave a small speech about the importance of jury duty and the pillars of democracy and the like. Then the bailiff escorted the jurors back to their jury room. Once they were inside gathering their things, the judge asked the lawyers if either side had anything further for the record. Raine certainly didn't. The prosecutor wasn't in a talkative mood either.

By the time the judge finally struck his gavel and ended the trial, it was 11:55. By the time Raine got back to the Medical Examiner's Office, it was 12:06. And they were closed for lunch.

Raine threw his hands up and cursed at the ceiling, but there was no one there to hear it.

He spent the next fifty-four minutes pacing the hallway and checking the time. The staff at the ME's Office might have needed to eat, but Raine's stomach was tied into a knot tight enough to repel even a sip of water. He didn't dare risk missing the receptionist if she came back early, but as it turned out, she was actually a few minutes late.

She stepped around the corner from the elevator bank at 1:03, key in hand, a few of her colleagues trailing behind her. "Oh, hello," she said upon seeing Raine. "You're that lawyer, right? Mr. Wilson, was it?"

"Mr. Raine," he corrected, trying to keep his voice measured. He had worked himself up into a bit of a mood while he'd waited. "Mr. Wilson was my client. Or his mother is, anyway."

The receptionist frowned. "Um, okay." She unlocked the door and stepped inside. "You wanted to see someone or something, right?"

"I wanted to make sure you didn't dispose of Mr. Wilson's body," Raine reminded her.

"Did you say Wilson?" one of the receptionist's coworkers asked. They had followed her into the office and were on their way through the interior door back to their desks, or examining tables, as might be the case. He was in his forties, clean shaven, with black hair pushed away from his face and square glasses with brown frames.

"Yes," Raine confirmed. "Thomas Wilson. Do you know anything about his autopsy or where his body is now?"

The man smiled. "I know a lot about both of those things. I'm Dr. Peter Nieuwendyk. I conducted the autopsy the morning he died. And his body was cremated just before lunch."

6

"Cremated?" Sawyer shook her head. "Oh man. That is not good. That is not good at all."

Raine frowned. "I'm aware of that."

After learning he had failed to preserve to best piece of evidence in both of his cases, Raine had been unable to bring himself to go back to the confines of his office. Instead, he'd opted for a long walk along the waterfront while he tried to forgive himself for having too many clients to serve all of them perfectly. The curse of being a solo practitioner, he told himself.

He'd called Sawyer to commiserate, and she'd suggested they do it over coffee. Everything seemed better over coffee. She had had an afternoon hearing on one of her own cases, so Raine turned around and headed to the courthouse. They'd met at the courthouse coffee shop. She even had his usual drink ready and on their table when he arrived.

Raine recounted what had happened, then stated the result. "Now there's no way to conduct an independent autopsy," he lamented. "We're stuck with whatever the ME says."

"And he's on the same payroll as the jail guards," Sawyer pointed out.

Raine could only nod at that. Dr. Peter Nieuwendyk seemed pleasant enough, but he didn't seem particularly curious either. He accepted Raine's explanation of his relationship to Tommy Wilson with barely more than a smile and noncommittal shrug. He didn't apologize for cremating the body because Ophelia had apparently agreed to that when she had signed off on the identification papers. And he declined to share his opinions as to Tommy's cause of death. He just crossed his arms and said, "I'm sure you'll know how to subpoena that once I've completed it."

"Well, he's not wrong," Sawyer remarked.

"Damn right he's not," Raine grumbled.

"So, what now?" Sawyer asked.

"Now?" Raine checked the time on his phone. "I need to finish my coffee and get over to the school. Jordan's play starts at four."

"Jordan's in the school play?" Sawyer beamed. "How cute! What is he? A tree? A tooth with a cavity?"

"He's thirteen, Sawyer, not five." Raine shook his head. "It's *Dracula*. He plays Jonathan Harker."

"Oh, so a bit role, huh?" Sawyer commiserated. "Well, I'm sure he'll make the most of whatever lines he has."

"It's one of the main roles in the play," Raine defended. "It's probably second only to Dracula himself."

"What about Van Helsing?" Sawyer asked. "He's a major character, right?"

"Well, yeah," Raine admitted. "But Harker is in almost

every scene. He's the one who hires Van Helsing. See, it's Harker's wife, Mina, Dracula wants—"

"I dunno, Dan," Sawyer interrupted. "I've heard of Van Helsing. I've never heard of Harker."

Raine realized she was yanking his chain. He leaned forward and grinned at her. "Well, you will after Jordan's performance today."

Sawyer laughed. "That's what I like to hear! Tell him good luck from me."

Raine hesitated. "Uh..."

Sawyer nodded. "Sitting with the ex, are you?"

"Well, he wanted us to be there," Raine explained. "Of course."

"Of course," Sawyer agreed. "Say hi to her too. Or don't. That's up to you."

Raine just nodded. It got awkward fast.

"Thanks," he decided to say after a moment. "And thanks for listening to me vent about letting the best piece of evidence in my case be destroyed."

"It might be a blessing in disguise," Sawyer suggested. "Maybe if you'd done a second autopsy, it just would have confirmed whatever the medical examiner said, and maybe that would have been something that hurt your case. Now, you'll be able to argue that the big bad government got rid of the evidence to cover up the truth."

"I suppose that's true," Raine agreed. "Not as good as proof that it was foul play, but better than proof it wasn't."

Sawyer raised her coffee cup triumphantly and took a drink.

"I sure do like talking shop with you," Raine admitted.

"And I like plays," Sawyer replied. "But don't worry. I'm not in any hurry."

Raine was glad for that too. As much as he liked Sawyer —and he liked her a lot—he wasn't looking to hurry into another serious relationship either.

———————

RAINE DID NEED to hurry to make it to the school on time. Traffic was unusually bad for a Monday afternoon before rush hour. There had been an accident on the main road to the school, so he'd been forced onto the side streets, and Seattle's side streets were rarely wide enough to fit more than one car at a time. He snaked his way through the neighborhoods and got to the school just in time to park in a fire lane, rush inside, and drop into the empty seat his ex-wife, Natalie, had saved for him.

"I was beginning to wonder whether you were going to show up," she whispered out of the corner of her mouth as the house lights began to dim.

Even in the dimming light, she looked as fantastic as the last time Raine had seen her. Simple yet elegant. Classy in a subdued way. Confident. Probably more so since the divorce. He felt bad for that.

"Wouldn't miss it for the world," he whispered back. He looked on the other side of Natalie, but the person there was a stranger. "Where's Jason?"

Natalie tipped her head toward the back of the theater. "Last row. He didn't want to sit with us."

"He didn't want to sit with me," Raine knew.

"Shh." Natalie avoided the conversation. "It's starting."

And so it was. With Jordan stepping out onto the stage and delivering a monologue of the letter Jonathan Harker wrote to Abraham Van Helsing, asking for his help with the mysterious stranger who had just moved into the home next door from his native Transylvania. Jordan's delivery was wonderful, and Raine melted into the moment of watching one of his children shine.

The play lasted almost two hours, including the fifteen-minute intermission. Raine had tracked down Jason, who acknowledged his father's presence, but little more. Raine's efforts to ask about classes, the lacrosse team, and girls were met with a series of monosyllabic replies and pained eye rolls. It wasn't much different from how they had interacted before the divorce, just more so. Raine could always chalk it up to Jason being in the very middle of his teenage years, so he went ahead and did that, even though they both knew it was more than that.

Raine returned to his seat a little early to have a moment to talk with Natalie, but she wasn't there. Her return coincided with the dimming of the lights, and Raine was left to wonder whether that was by design.

The second act was even better than the first. Jordan didn't manage to steal the show from the kids playing Dracula and Van Helsing, but he held his own. Not bad for an eighth grader in his first dramatic role. He had a future in the high school drama club.

After the play, Raine milled about the lobby, waiting for Jordan to come out. He managed some small talk with Natalie, but nothing significant. Just about how well Jordan had done and specific scenes they especially liked.

Jordan finally appeared, still sweaty from the stage lights, and rushed to give his mom a hug. Then he saw his dad and gave him a hug too. "Thanks for coming!" he gushed. "How did you like it?"

"It was fantastic," Raine answered enthusiastically.

"*You* were fantastic," Natalie added, almost a correction. She handed Jordan a single rose she had kept hidden in her coat. "Bravo."

Raine's hands had never felt emptier. But he resisted the urge to explain why he hadn't brought flowers. "What was your favorite part?" he asked his son. After all, it was his night.

"Oh my God, there was so much that was awesome," Jordan answered with the broadest smile Raine had seen on him since the divorce. "The end scene, though? In the basement of the castle? That was amazing. Did you notice that Aiden messed up his line? I totally covered for him and got him back on track. Did you guys notice that?"

"No," Natalie answered. "Not at all."

"Good job." Raine patted him on the shoulder.

Then Jordan craned his neck to look past his parents. "There's Jason. I gotta see how he liked it." And before either Raine or Natalie could say anything, he was gone.

"Well, that sure is nice," Raine offered after a moment. "It's great to see him so excited about something."

"It's great to see him happy," Natalie said, in what again felt like a correction.

"He really did do a great job." Raine started to recycle the topics from before Jordan came out from backstage.

"Yes, he did," Natalie agreed. She was looking after where Jordan had disappeared, not at her ex-husband.

"And it's nice that he wants his brother to be here too," Raine observed.

"Yes, it is."

Raine wanted to say it was nice to have the family back together again. And it was. To a point. But it wasn't the same. And he knew that too. So he didn't say it. He missed what they had been, but they weren't that anymore. He didn't feel like being reminded of it.

"I'm going to go ahead and say goodbye to the boys, then," he announced. "I'll pick them up Friday at the usual time."

"Sounds good, Dan." Natalie finally turned to look at him. "It was good to see you. Thanks for coming."

It was good to see Natalie too. He didn't say that either.

7

R aine next set about the business of getting Ophelia's two cases off the ground. Or rather getting the civil case off the ground and preparing to defend against the criminal case, which was being put off the ground not by him, but rather by the King County Prosecutor's Office. The same people, it turned out, who would be defending the civil lawsuit.

The county prosecutor's office was responsible for all of the legal matters a county might have to deal with. One division—the largest section—dealt with prosecuting criminal cases. But another, smaller division dealt with civil matters. Taxation and zoning, labor contracts and sidewalk easements. And perhaps most importantly, at least to Raine and Ophelia Wilson, the civil division defended the county against lawsuits, like wrongful death claims. That meant the criminal attorney who was prosecuting Ophelia worked for the same boss as the civil attorney who was defending against Ophelia's case. In theory, the cases should be handled separately. In practice, they would be joined at the hip. The hips of criminal Deputy District Attorney Catherine Tennet and civil Deputy District Attorney Jackson Pierce.

Raine hadn't dealt with either of them before. Avoiding criminal cases meant avoiding prosecutors, and Raine hadn't sued the county civilly since he was a baby lawyer and filed a discrimination claim for a janitor who thought he was let go for being too old. It turned out that client was also chronically late, did slipshod work, and drank on the job. Raine had taken his third of the nominal settlement offer the county presented to make the case go away—"nuisance value" was what the lawyers called it—and never found himself retained to take on the county again until Ophelia hired him all these years later.

Raine would meet Tennet first, at the pretrial on the criminal case. Pretrials were usually scheduled two weeks after the arraignment, so it had been two weeks since Raine had successfully argued for Ophelia's release from jail, and almost three weeks since her son had died inside that same jail. He would meet Pierce next, at the first depositions in the civil case, already scheduled for a week after the criminal trial. That would give the two of them plenty of time to coordinate their attacks.

"Drop the civil case, and I'll give your gal a misdemeanor," Tennet began the negotiations the morning of the pretrial. She had thick brown hair cut into a wavy bob, and wore the same nondescript dark suit all the prosecutors wore. She had a pleasant face, although in that moment it held a distinctly unpleasant expression. "Pick one. Resisting. Trespassing. Disorderly. Whatever you think best describes her conduct."

"I think," Raine responded in a measured tone, "that

none of those crimes describe her conduct. Because she didn't commit a crime."

Tennet sighed and looked around the room.

They were in a large negotiation room filled with prosecutors and defense attorneys. It was like a speed-dating event. Tennet probably had several other cases set for pretrial that morning. After she finished talking to Raine, she would go find the next defense attorney, who even then was talking to a different prosecutor about a different case. Some of them, especially the public defenders with the crushing caseloads, would likely be there all morning. Raine just had the one case. He was in no hurry to resolve the case.

"Look." Tennet put her hands on her hips. She was standing over him, eschewing the empty chair at the table Raine was seated at. "I get it. Your lady, she had a bad day."

"Her son was killed," Raine pointed out.

"Right," Tennet acknowledged.

"In the jail."

"Yeah."

"And no one would tell her what happened."

"Well, I don't know about that part." Tennet raised her palm at the suggestion. "But I do know that none of that is an excuse to break the law."

"Which gets us back to the fact that she didn't break the law," Raine said. "You've heard of the Constitution, right? Freedom of speech and all that. She can protest her son's murder."

"Whoa, whoa." Tennet's other palm joined the first. "No one said anything about murder."

"I just did," Raine pointed out.

"You're not going to get to tell the jury that," Tennet warned.

"I'm pretty sure you're wrong about that," Raine replied. "But I'm glad to see you're thinking about the trial. Because this case is going to trial unless you dismiss it."

Tennet sighed again. She finally sat down across from Raine. "You know I can't dismiss this case. The cops would go ballistic."

"They already went ballistic," Raine answered, "on my client."

"Let's not resort to hyperbole." Tennet shook her head. "That won't solve anything. Your client believes she didn't do anything, so she wants a dismissal. My cops think she was way out of line and endangered them and their ability to do their jobs to protect the public. You and me? We're just stuck in the middle. They say a good compromise is one where both sides are disappointed. Your gal will be disappointed to get a misdemeanor on her record. My cops will be disappointed that's all she got. Lose-lose for them, but win-win for you and me. So what do you say? Wrap this up in one court hearing and spend that retainer money on a nice date with the wife."

They both looked down at Raine's ring finger.

"Or girlfriend," Tennet amended. "Or boyfriend. Whatever. You know what I mean."

"I know what you mean," Raine answered. "I'm just surprised you said it out loud."

"Negotiations are about offers and counteroffers," Tennet defended. "All I did was offer her a misdemeanor."

"Not that." Raine waved his hand. "The part about having to drop the civil suit as part of any plea bargain."

"Well, of course." Tennet sat up a bit straighter. "I mean, if she pleads guilty to disorderly conduct or even trespassing, your civil case will get torpedoed anyway."

"I know." Raine nodded. "That's another reason she won't be pleading guilty to anything."

Tennet took several moments before sighing again and standing up. "Fine. No deals, then. Your poor mother can get convicted of multiple felonies and go off to prison. I'm the only thing standing between her and that fate. Let me know if you change your mind."

"There's one more thing standing between Ophelia Wilson and prison," Raine said.

"What's that?" Tennet asked.

Raine finally stood up and squared his shoulders at his opponent. "Me."

8

Raine actually liked Catherine Tennet. She seemed prepared and professional. She also seemed to understand the general weakness of her position, factually if not morally. She would be a worthy opponent and one he would enjoy defeating.

So he was a bit surprised when he arrived for the first set of depositions in the civil case a full week after the criminal trial and Tennet's colleague seemed to be completely uninformed as to how the criminal negotiations had gone.

"Are we still doing this?" Jackson Pierce asked. "Catherine said the civil case was going to be dismissed. She said she was going to make you an offer you couldn't refuse."

Raine shrugged. "I refused it."

They were at the offices for the Civil Division of the King County Prosecutor's Office. Unlike the criminal division, which was inside the courthouse, the civil division was housed a few blocks away in just another one of Seattle's downtown office towers. It might have been any other private law firm in the city save for the county seal on the glass of the main entrance.

Jackson Pierce also seemed like he belonged more to a private law firm than a government agency. He wore a tailored suit in a unique but understated pattern, with highly polished shoes and a colorful silk tie. His hair was styled in a sharp fade, and his smile was broad and bright. It disappeared for a moment at Raine's comment.

"Well, that is going to be disappointing to my corrections officers," Pierce remarked. "They are very nervous. They aren't commissioned police officers. They're jail guards. They aren't used to being questioned by a defense attorney."

Raine wasn't surprised to hear that. It was customary for the witness to come to the office of the attorney conducting the deposition, but they had balked at going to Raine's office. Raine wasn't into needless power games, so he'd agreed to do the depositions at the prosecutor's office. But apparently, they were still nervous. *Good.*

"So who do you want to start with?" Pierce asked. "Porter or Frazier?"

"No counteroffer?" Raine inquired. "Like, plead guilty to the criminal case and we'll give you ten grand to go away?"

"What? Oh, no." Pierce shook his head quickly at the suggestion. "No, of course not. Catherine can try to help me, but I'm not looking to help her. I have a job to do. And so do you. Let's do it. Porter or Frazier?"

Raine couldn't have cared less. They were the two guards who were supposed to be watching Tommy when he died. Which one they spoke to first wouldn't make a bit of difference.

"Let's go alphabetically," Raine suggested. "Porter first."

"Excellent decision," Pierce complimented him. He

gestured toward an empty conference room on the other side of the lobby. "We'll be in there. I'll go fetch Porter from the waiting room."

"Is Frazier with him?" Raine asked, though he already knew the answer.

"Yes."

"So they've had time to collude on their stories," Raine pointed out.

"Oh, Dan." Pierce laughed. "You and I both know they did that weeks ago. At most, they were going over the finer details this morning."

It was meant as a joke, but one of those jokes that's funny because it's true. From the moment Porter and Frazier found Tommy dead in his cell, they had undoubtedly been working on their cover story for why it wasn't their fault.

Raine didn't expect either of them to confess to anything, but they were going to be witnesses at the trial, and in the world of civil litigation, you deposed every witness before they got up in front of the jury. You wanted to know every last thing they were going to say, and have the transcript to make them say it again if they deviated. It was cumbersome, but it paid the bills. Or it would if he won.

Raine strolled into the conference room and took stock of the space. It was larger than his. A dozen people would easily have fit around the table. It had a nice view too. Twenty stories up and facing the water. Although Elliott Bay was hard to see through the rain beating against the window just then. It was a gray day. Perfect for spending hours talking to jail guards.

Pierce returned not only with a uniformed man Raine could reasonably conclude was Porter, but also a woman carrying a stenography machine. The court reporter who would take down every word so they had that transcript if they really did need it at the trial.

In short order, everyone was seated around the table. Porter and Pierce on one side. Raine opposite them. The court reporter between them, at the head of the table.

"Before we get started"—Pierce spoke up and looked to Porter—"this is Mr. Raine's deposition. He will be asking the questions. You may have seen on television where lawyers yell at each other and object and generally obstruct each other during a deposition. That is fiction. In truth, I can make an objection if I think the answer Mr. Raine is trying to elicit won't be admissible at trial, but then you go ahead and answer the question anyway. Later on, if a judge agrees with my objection, then we excise your answer. But today, you answer. I just don't want you to think I'm not doing my job if I end up sitting here and listening most of the time. Are you going to be okay with that?"

Porter appeared disappointed, but he shrugged. "Sure."

"I'm okay with it," Raine added. "It should help these go quickly."

Although Raine wondered if that wasn't Pierce's actual strategy. He wasn't being deferential just because it was professionally appropriate, or even because it was easier. He was doing it because he thought he would gain from it. At least, that was why Raine would have done it.

The court reporter swore Porter in, getting him to affirm that he would tell the truth, the whole truth, and nothing but the truth.

Then Raine began. "Please state your full name for the record."

"Kyle Oliver Porter," was the response.

Raine followed that most basic of questions with a few

more, in part to gather the information in case it was needed later, but also just to get Porter to start talking and relax a little bit. Raine wanted him relaxed enough to accidentally tell the truth when Pierce wasn't watching. So Raine had Porter provide his date of birth, home address, and of course, current employment.

"I'm a corrections officer at the King County Correctional Facility."

"The King County Jail?" Raine translated the official name of the building to the name everyone actually called it.

"Yes," Porter agreed.

"How long have you been a corrections officer at the King County Jail?" Raine asked.

"It'll be one year at the end of next month," Porter answered.

Raine's eyebrows rose slightly. "So less than a year into your job and you had to deal with a dead inmate?"

One of the tricks of asking strangers questions they didn't want to answer was to figure out a way to make it about them. Everyone loves talking about themselves. Instead of starting with what happened to Tommy, Raine started with how it made Porter feel.

"Yes, well," Porter stammered, "I guess that's part of the job sometimes too. It was bound to happen eventually."

Raine offered a nod in agreement. "Let's talk about what led up to that, shall we? What were your duties that shift?"

"I was main watch on Three-West," Porter answered. He translated, "Third floor, west wing. It was me and Frazier that shift."

"How many inmates are housed on that wing?" Raine asked.

"Thirty," Porter answered. "There are three pods of ten inmates each."

"And cells for solitary confinement," Raine reminded more than asked. Tommy had died in one of the solitary cells.

"Yes," Porter agreed. His expression showed he knew why it was important.

"Tommy Wilson ended up in one of those solitary confinement cells, didn't he?" Raine asked.

"Yes, he did," Porter confirmed.

"Do you know why?" Raine followed up. "Aren't those usually for inmates who pose a safety concern to themselves or other inmates?"

"Sometimes," Porter agreed.

"Was Tommy a threat to himself or the other inmates?" Raine asked.

Porter shrugged. "I don't know. I don't make classification decisions. He was in there when we started our shift. It was our job to check on him at regular intervals, which we did."

"Until you found him dead," Raine said.

"Yes," Porter agreed.

"What time was that?" Raine asked.

"It was zero-five-twenty," Porter reported in the military convention the cops also used.

"Five twenty in the morning," Raine translated. "Please describe what you saw."

So Porter did. Tommy was sprawled out, facedown, in the center of the cell. There was no sign of self-harm, and no one else was in the cell, since it was solitary. Frazier checked for vital signs while Porter called for medical aid. The jail medics arrived and tried to resuscitate him, but to no avail.

He was dead. So the next call Porter made was to the Medical Examiner's Office to come collect the body.

"And you have no idea how he might have died?" Raine asked.

"None, sir," Porter answered. "There wasn't anything that obviously caused his death. I'm not even sure what he died from."

Raine wasn't either. The Medical Examiner's Office was slow-walking their compliance with Raine's subpoena for the autopsy report.

"Do you want to hazard a guess?" Raine invited.

"Guess what he died from?" Porter shook his head. "No, sir. I'm sure I would be wrong, but I'm also sure it would create some kind of issue in this lawsuit if I guessed. I'll stick with being a corrections officer. That's enough for me."

It was enough for Raine too.

"I don't think I have any more questions for Officer Porter," he informed Pierce. "How about we take a fifteen-minute break and then start with Officer Frazier?"

Pierce agreed with the suggestion.

A few minutes later Raine found himself alone again in the conference room. He still couldn't see Elliott Bay for the weather. The rain had gotten worse during Porter's deposition, pattering loudly on the glass as they conducted the question-and-answer session. It was going to be a wet walk back to the office if it didn't clear up by the time he was finished with Frazier.

After the break, Pierce fetched Frazier, and everyone took the same seats around the table, meaning Frazier took Porter's seat. Taking up the same space that Porter had been in for several hours underscored Frazier's significantly larger size than Porter, who was not a small man himself. Raine suspected Frazier was probably used to being the largest person in any room he was in save perhaps some professional sporting events.

Frazier also wore a considerably less friendly countenance than Porter. The first deposition had been conversational, pleasant even. Raine had learned some things, and as Pierce predicted, no one needed to yell over anyone else. Frazier, on the other hand, locked a scowl onto Raine from the moment he plodded into the conference room. Raine knew how to deal with an adverse witness, but that didn't mean he was going to enjoy it. Plus, it was going to take far longer. More time for the rain to let up, he supposed.

The court reporter swore Frazier in, and Raine began. "Please state your full name for the record."

And Frazier began as well. "Why do you need my full name?"

Raine turned to Pierce. "Are we really going to do this?"

Pierce just shrugged. "I don't want to be accused of coaching my witnesses. This is your deposition. I'm sure you'll figure it out."

Raine looked to the court reporter. "Please indicate that the deponent refused to answer the question."

Frazier frowned at that. Whatever else he was, professionally he was a rule enforcer. He didn't like being reported on.

"What's your date of birth?" Raine didn't look up from his list of questions.

"Why do you—?" Frazier started.

"Please indicate that the deponent refused to answer the next question as well." Raine finally looked up at Frazier. "We can do this all day if you want. And then I'll show the transcript to the judge, and the judge will order you to do the deposition again, even though a lawyer is only supposed to depose a given witness one time. You will double the amount of your time this wastes, and you will, eventually, answer my questions anyway."

Frazier stared at Raine for several long seconds. Pierce didn't say anything. The court reporter didn't even breathe.

Finally, Frazier pushed himself back in his chair and crossed his arms. "William Alexander Frazier. June 17, 1991."

And they were off. Raine knew not to smile on the outside, but he was definitely smiling on the inside as he led William Alexander Frazier through his job title, job duties, and employment history. He'd been a corrections officer for almost ten years. That sounded impressive, but Raine thought it more likely meant that he had failed to land a job as a commissioned police officer in that time. A lot of cops started as jail guards to get their foot in the door. Porter would probably be a regular cop in another year or two. Frazier, apparently not.

Then Raine got to the morning in question. "You were working a shift with Officer Porter that day, correct?"

"Correct," Frazier fairly conceded. He was answering the questions, but his tone remained defiant.

"Three-West?"

"Correct."

"Thirty inmates in three pods of ten, right?" Raine said.

"Plus solitary confinement cells," Frazier volunteered.

It was basically the same interview as before. "And Tommy Wilson died in one of those solitary confinement cells, didn't he?"

"Yes," Frazier said. "He was placed in there after he initiated a physical altercation with the arresting officer prior to his arrival at the facility."

Or maybe it wasn't the same interview. "What time did he arrive?"

"Just after midnight," Frazier answered.

"So he was placed in solitary during your shift?"

"Yes," Frazier answered.

"Are you the one who personally put him in the cell?" Raine asked.

Frazier thought for a moment before replying, the first time he'd done so the entire deposition. "Yes."

Raine took a moment himself. Then he decided to go back to the script. The rest of Frazier's answers mirrored those of Porter. Checked on him at 0520 hours. Nonresponsive. Medical aid was called but couldn't revive him. Eventually called the Medical Examiner's Office to collect the body. Went back to work.

Raine thanked both Frazier and the court reporter and then stared out the window while he waited for Pierce to come back from escorting them out.

"A full day of depositions." Pierce clapped his hands together upon his return. "Are you sure you don't want to take Catherine's offer after all?"

"It wasn't much of an offer," Raine replied. "Dismiss your case and plead guilty on hers."

"To a misdemeanor," Pierce reminded him.

"To a crime," Raine reminded right back. "What can you offer independent of the criminal case?"

Pierce chuckled. "At this point, nothing. I mean, maybe a nuisance value payment in the neighborhood of ten thousand dollars. But I would have to get approval of even that. And I'm sure they would connect it to some sort of plea on the criminal case."

"Those cases should be separate," Raine responded as he turned away from the window.

"Are you planning on keeping them separate?" Pierce challenged. "I'm sure you'll tell the criminal jury that the county was responsible for the death of your client's son. And I'm sure you'll tell the civil jury that your client was unlawfully arrested in retaliation for her protests."

"She was," Raine insisted.

Pierce shrugged. "Who really knows?"

"Well, one thing we do know is that your guards aren't going to help you any," Raine said. "One of them is lying."

"I think that might be a bit of a stretch," Pierce cautioned. "People remember things differently. That doesn't mean one of them is lying."

"There is one other possibility," Raine suggested.

"What's that?" Pierce cocked his head inquisitively.

"They're both lying."

9

The autopsy report arrived three days later. It was about as helpful as Raine expected. Less, in fact.

He expected Dr. Nieuwendyk to claim a cause of death that would absolve the county of responsibility. Maybe a drug overdose, something like that. But instead, the good doctor listed the cause of death as "Natural Causes— Other." He posited it might have had something to do with the trace amounts of drugs in his system but couldn't say for sure. Then he'd signed the report and burned the body.

There was nothing for an independent expert to attack, even if they hired one to critique the official autopsy report. Tommy Wilson was dead. That much was established. Everything else was guesswork.

"Why the long face?" came a voice from his office doorframe.

Raine looked up from his desk to see Rebecca Sommers darkening his doorway. She was dressed in a white skirt suit, perfectly tailored, with three-inch platform shoes and her long platinum hair falling loose down her back. Her usual appearance: flawless and striking. It had been a while since Raine had seen her; he hadn't really had any cases that had called for her particular skill set as a private investigator.

"Somebody die?" Sommers finished her question.

"Actually, yes." Raine waved the autopsy report in the air. "My newest client's son. But I don't know how. Or why. Not yet anyway."

"That's the spirit," Rebecca complimented Raine's last sentiment. She stepped into the office and sat in the chair opposite him. "We'll figure it out together."

Sommers was a commercial real estate agent by actual profession. Private investigator was more of a hobby, although she had proved herself more than capable at it. But those cases had involved rich clients and multimillion-dollar penthouses. Not a dead drug addict in a jail cell.

"I'm not sure this is the kind of case you would be interested in," Raine said. "No fancy condos or business leads. Just a dead kid and a grieving mother."

"Kid?" Sommers gasped.

"Well, young adult," Raine corrected. "But his mother is still grieving. She's also facing multiple felonies for daring to try to bring attention to her son's death while in the care of the county jail."

"Really?" Sommers leaned back in the chair and placed a thoughtful hand to her chin. "Tell me more."

So Raine did. He explained both cases, from his first glimpse of Ophelia in front of the jail, through the pretrial and depositions, to the unhelpful autopsy report. When he finished, he shrugged at her. "See, not really your kind of case."

Sommers leaned forward. "Don't tell me what kind of case is mine. This sounds important. I want to help."

"Everything I do is important," Raine asserted.

But Sommers raised an eyebrow at the claim.

"Well, maybe not everything," Raine admitted. "Do you really want to work on these? It won't be glamorous."

"I'm glamorous enough on my own," Sommers only half joked as she ran a hand through her luxurious hair. "I'm ready for something a little more challenging."

"I'm not sure if it'll be more challenging," Raine cautioned, "but I'm sure there's something we can have you do."

Raine thought for a moment. Then a few more. Then even more. "You know, I'm not exactly sure what I would even need you to do on this one." He considered the autopsy report still in his hand. "You don't happen to have a real estate client who's a forensic pathologist, do you?"

"Probably," Sommers answered dismissively. She stood up, clearly energized at the prospect of whatever she was about to do. "Don't worry. I have a better idea."

"Oh really?" Raine was surprised. "What?"

"I'll tell you after I do it," Sommers answered. "Talk to you soon."

Raine tried to call out after her about how it was the attorney who should be making the decisions that drive the case, but she was out of earshot and out of the office before he could say anything more than, "Well, actually..."

He wasn't excited about Sommers out there on her own doing whatever crazy thing she had planned. But he was excited to see how it worked out.

"PORTER," Sommers announced two days later when she again appeared in Raine's office doorway uninvited and unexpected.

"I'm sorry, what?" Raine looked up from the file he was reading. Sommers was again dressed like she was about to show a penthouse condominium to a venture capitalist. She probably was, after she told Raine whatever she had come to tell him.

"Not what," Sommers corrected. "Who. Kyle Porter, the jail guard. He's your target."

"My target?" Raine asked. "My target for what?"

"For figuring out what really happened to Tommy Wilson," Sommers answered. "Because he didn't just die by himself for no reason. If you can find out who did it and why, you'll win both cases. And Corrections Officer Kyle Porter is going to help you."

"Why him?" Raine asked. "I already deposed him. If you ask me, that Frazier guy was a lot more suspicious. I didn't like him one bit."

"You're going to like Porter less when you hear what I found out about him," Sommers promised. She sat down in the chair across from Raine's desk. "You ready?"

Raine supposed he was. He set aside the file. "Hit me."

"What does a first-year corrections officer make?" Sommers asked.

Raine sighed. It was going to be the Socratic method. Fine. He could do that. "I'm not sure."

"Not much," Sommers answered. "It's a public-sector job, so the salaries for every job classification are posted. It only took a few minutes to figure out his salary."

"So how much does he make?" Raine went ahead and asked.

"Not enough to afford his new car," Sommers answered. "Or the apartment downtown he just moved into. And definitely not enough to lose all of the money I watched him lose at the casino last night."

"You followed him?" Raine laughed.

"Please." Sommers drew herself up haughtily. "I'm a private investigator. I tailed him."

"Nice." Raine nodded approvingly. "How much did he lose?"

"Hundreds," Sommers answered. "More than a thousand, I think. It was hard to tell because he was betting almost randomly, throwing money at any table that was open."

"Sounds reckless," Raine observed.

"It's reckless if it's your money," Sommers said. "It's entertainment if it's someone else's."

"Whose?" Raine asked. But then answered his own question. "Whoever paid him off to cover up what really happened to Tommy."

"That was my conclusion too," Sommers said. "Pretty good for someone you thought could only work high-value cases, huh? And I can assure you, that casino, the one out on Lake City Way right at the city limit? That place is definitely not high end."

Raine knew the casino she meant. It was a bit of a Seattle institution, but it was a far cry from the glass and steel skyscrapers downtown.

He considered the time, then decided there was no time like the present. "I think I need to have another conversation with Kyle Porter. One without the county's attorney present."

"You shouldn't go alone," Sommers said. "If nothing else, you should have a witness whenever you talk to someone who might claim something crazy later. You taught me that the day we met."

Raine smiled at the memory. "I did, didn't I? All right then. Let's go talk with Officer Porter. I need you to show me where his new luxury apartment is anyway."

Sommers offered a small fist pump. "I knew there'd be a real estate angle somehow."

10

Porter had rented an apartment at the Harbor Steps, an upscale complex on Western Avenue where Seneca Street converted from a standard roadway to pedestrian steps down to the waterfront, the tourist area of the city. It was a nicer part of downtown than up on Third Avenue or over by Belltown. No homeless encampments. They kept it clean.

It had been a desirable address since it first opened decades earlier. Since then, rent increases had only accelerated. It might have been nice to live in a city where a public servant could afford an apartment like the ones at Harbor Steps. But Seattle wasn't that city.

"I've always liked these," Raine commented as they arrived at the base of the stylishly cut cement steps. "I even thought about renting here when Natalie and I separated."

"Why didn't you?" Sommers asked.

Raine looked up at the glass and steel high-rise with unobstructed views of Elliott Bay and the Olympic Mountains beyond. "I couldn't afford it."

"You need a side hustle," Sommers suggested. "Like moonlighting as a private investigator."

"Or covering up murders in the jail," Raine replied.

"So you really think it was murder?" Sommers asked.

Raine nodded at the entrance to the apartment tower. "I'm beginning to. You don't pay someone off if it really was an accident."

The front door to the lobby was unlocked. Raine pulled it open for his companion, and they walked inside.

In lieu of locked doors, there was a concierge's desk, with a woman in a beige blazer sitting behind it. Raine guessed she had a button on her desk that would summon private security into the lobby in a matter of seconds. Just because the neighborhood was nicer didn't mean it was perfect.

"Hello," the concierge greeted them. She had her hair pulled into a bun and bright red lipstick. "How can I help you?"

"Let me do the talking," Sommers whispered to Raine.

Raine wasn't sure he needed to let Sommers take the lead. They were trying to find a specific resident, not schmooze a room full of real estate developers. But he didn't suppose it would hurt either. It might even be entertaining. "Sure."

"Hello," Sommers effused. "My name is Rebecca Sommers. I'm an award-winning real estate agent here in our fair city, and this is my assistant, Mr. Raine. We were wondering whether you might be able to help us get in contact with a resident here, a certain Mr.—"

"Kyle Porter!" Raine shouted when he saw Porter emerge from the elevator bank across the brightly decorated lobby.

Porter froze at the sound of his name. He took a moment

to size up Raine. A flash of recognition crossed his face. Then he bolted for the exit at the side of the lobby.

Raine sprinted after him.

He heard Sommers offer some sort of apology for his behavior, but he was focused on catching Porter before he disappeared into the city streets. The side door led to Post Alley and from there Union Street. If Raine didn't keep up, he'd lose him in the tourist foot traffic either heading west to the waterfront or east to the shopping district.

The lobby door was swinging closed as Raine reached it. He slammed it back open with all of his weight and pushed off the threshold into a full sprint. Porter had several hundred feet on him already, and unlike Raine, he wasn't wearing a suit and dress shoes.

Luckily there were plenty of tourists milling about Post Alley, in no hurry and generally wandering aimlessly around the carless street. Porter was slowed as he dodged his way through the young couples and sprawling families and old women, none of whom reacted well to his efforts to avoid them. Raine was able to draft in Porter's wake, but Porter was the icebreaker crashing against the floes.

By the time Porter reached Union, Raine was almost caught up to him. Porter wasted another moment deciding which way to turn, then dashed to his left, toward the waterfront. Raine smiled. There were only two blocks until Porter ran out of real estate, and an extremely busy Alaskan Way thoroughfare before then as well. Porter wasn't going to get away from him.

Unless Porter was dumb enough—or desperate enough —to jump in front of moving traffic on Alaskan Way. Even then, Porter bore the brunt of that interaction, slowing him down as he made efforts not to be killed by a car. Raine

benefited from the cars already having stopped by the time
he reached the curb. When they reached the other curb, he
was within an arm's reach of Porter.

"What are you doing?" Raine shouted. "I know where
you work. I can find you. Why are you running?"

Porter turned around and raised his fists as he pedaled
backward. "I can't talk to you again. I can't be seen talking to
you."

"Well, you've made it pretty hard for people not to look at
us," Raine observed, bearing down on him. He didn't feel a
need to raise his own fists. Porter was exhausted. He could
take him if it came to that. But it already would have come to
that if it were going to. "There isn't a person on the waterfront who isn't watching the crazy guy who ran into traffic
and the crazier guy following him."

It was true. Everyone within sight was stopped and
staring at them. Two grown men about to have a fistfight on
the Seattle Waterfront? That was more interesting than
whatever they were selling inside that T-shirt and curios
"shoppe."

"Why don't we ratchet this down a notch or two?" Raine
suggested. "I just want to ask you a couple of follow-up
questions."

"I can't be seen talking to you," Porter repeated, glancing
around. He finally stopped, but he kept his fists up. "That's
why they put me up in the Harbor Steps. So they could
watch me. They can't see me talking to you."

"Who?" Raine asked. He stopped as well. Porter was
genuinely frightened. Panicked even. As long as they were
close enough to talk, that was close enough for Raine.

"I can't tell you," Porter answered. "It's too much." He
looked around. "It's too late."

Raine considered the situation. Porter was barely rational. He needed to feel safe before he would say anything, and he clearly had something to say. There weren't really any private areas on the Waterfront. That was sort of the entire point of the Waterfront. It was for tourists looking for things to do. Harbor cruises and Ferris wheel rides. They needed to get across Alaskan Way and—

"Dan!" Sommers ran up to him, out of breath and very, very loud. "What's going on? Did you catch him? You caught him! Is he the murderer? Did he confess?"

"Murderer?" Porter shrieked. "How do you know he was murdered?"

Words were funny things. Important things. Subtle variations could completely change the meaning of something and the conclusions to be drawn from it. Raine didn't notice any of that then because of what happened next. Porter jumped back into traffic and directly in front of an oncoming semitruck.

11

The driver of the truck had no chance to stop. Porter's body made a wet cracking thump of a sound as it bounced first off the vehicle's grille, then off the pavement, and finally came to rest some thirty feet away. Any doubt he was dead was quickly dispelled by the amount of blood pouring out of his open skull.

"Oh my God!" Sommers shouted through the hands she raised over her mouth.

Raine just frowned. It was too late for Porter. And it was too late for them to find out what he might have told them. He was tempted to leave before the cops came, but given the circumstances, he didn't want to graduate from witness to suspect based on his departure. There were plenty of other witnesses who had seen Raine talking, one might even say "arguing," with Porter. To suddenly leave might lead to speculation that Porter was pushed, and speculation was one of those things that was hard to gain control over once it started. Especially if you weren't there when it started.

Sommers elected to remain as well, if only to support

Raine's story. Which would be easy. It would be the truth. Most of it, anyway. Raine could hardly claim he wasn't the lawyer who had deposed Porter days earlier. Sometimes the truth was the best approach. Not always, but sometimes. Even with the police.

They waited while the first responders arrived, then while the scene was cordoned off, then while the forensics and accident reconstruction teams arrived. The detective was usually the last to arrive, and he had to check in with all of his colleagues before he started talking to the witnesses.

"Good morning," the detective finally greeted them. "I'm Detective Leo Gillespie. I understand you two witnessed what happened?"

Gillespie was in his forties, with a thick build and fat hands. He hadn't shaved that day and could have used a haircut. He generally looked like he wasn't taking care of himself as much as he should, which seemed to be a common problem for cops in their forties.

Raine nodded. They were sitting on the curb of Alaskan Way, near but not too near to where Porter met his untimely, and untidy, end. He decided to stand up. Sommers didn't.

"Yes," Raine confirmed. He extended his hand. "Daniel Raine. I'm an attorney. This is my investigator Rebecca Sommers. We were actually trying to speak with Officer Porter when he stepped in front of the truck that struck him."

"He must have really not wanted to talk to you," Gillespie joked. When Raine didn't laugh, he apologized. "Sorry. Dark humor. Comes with the job, unfortunately. What were you talking to him about?"

So Raine explained. Most of it. Tommy's death. His mother's arrest and criminal charges. The civil suit. The deposition. He left out the new car and the casino losses. That was also speculation. "I thought of a few more questions I wanted to ask him, so we came down to his apartment to see if he had a few minutes to talk."

Gillespie frowned. "You didn't go through his attorney?"

"Well, Mr. Pierce wasn't his attorney," Raine explained. "That attorney represents the county. Officer Porter was just a witness, not a named defendant to the lawsuit."

Gillespie nodded. "How did you end up at the Waterfront?"

"Ah, yes," Raine hesitated. "Good question."

"He wanted some privacy." Sommers stood up and answered. "When we met him in the lobby of his apartment building, he didn't want to talk there. He led us here."

True, yet misleading, Raine admired.

"And sorry, what were you talking about again?" Gillespie repeated his question.

"Just some follow-up." Raine didn't quite answer. "You know, lawyer stuff."

Gillespie frowned. "I'm not sure I do. I'm not a lawyer. I have to work with them a lot, but that doesn't mean I understand them." He glanced around at the other emergency personnel and witnesses standing at the scene. "I'm hearing this guy didn't just step into traffic. He jumped. While he was talking to you. So I'll ask one more time, what were you talking about?"

Raine glanced at Sommers, who returned his look. "Like I said, lawyer stuff. I don't always know what my next question will be until I hear the answer to the last one. His version of events didn't quite match up with the other guard's, and he had left by the time we'd finished the other guard's deposition. Usually, people don't lie. They just remember differently. I figured he'd be able to explain it away, and I didn't want to waste time on a discrepancy that was an honest mistake and not a cover-up."

Gillespie considered Raine's answer for several moments, then let out a long sigh. "And then he jumped in front of a truck?"

Raine nodded. "Apparently."

"What was the last question you asked him?" Gillespie pressed.

"I asked him if he'd be willing to answer a few more questions."

"I guess not," Sommers put in. Then, "Sorry. Dark humor. Comes with the job."

Gillespie sighed again. "Fine. I'll let you two go. But I'll be in touch if this turns out to be more than just an accident."

Raine felt certain of both of those things. He'd see Gillespie again. And Porter's death was more than an accident.

12

"We need his bank statements," Sommers declared when they got back to Raine's office. He dropped himself in his desk chair; Sommers sat down opposite him. "And his credit card statements. The sales agreement for that car. Oh, and the apartment lease. I bet someone cosigned."

"I doubt the people paying him off cosigned his lease," Raine opined. "It would defeat the purpose of keeping things quiet."

"Maybe." Sommers shrugged, arms crossed and chin raised. "But people do stupid things. That's why you have a job."

Raine supposed that was true. "We could get all of those things, probably. But it would take time. And a lot of paper and daylight. I would have to get the judge to sign off on the subpoenas, and there's no guarantee they would. Porter wasn't a defendant. He was just a witness. Plenty of witnesses do shady stuff in their personal lives. Again, that's why I have a job. It doesn't mean we get access to it."

"It does if he lied in his deposition about what happened to your client the day he died," Sommers argued.

"Maybe," Raine allowed. "But again, I'm going to have to put all of that in writing and then argue it out loud again in open court. The people behind this are going to know we're onto something. They scatter and we never figure out what really happened to Tommy."

"So what's the alternative?" Sommers pushed her fists onto her hips. "Do nothing?"

"Of course not," Raine answered. He pushed himself out of his desk chair. "Think of it like a building, and the information we need is inside. If we knock on the front door, everyone knows we're there, there's no guarantee we get invited inside, and even if we do, they'll be watching our every move. But if we have a key to the back door, we can be in and out with the information we need without anyone knowing we were ever there."

"I like the real estate angle," Sommers allowed, "but I have no idea what you're talking about. Who has a back door to what house?"

"Tommy is the back door," Raine answered.

Sommers nodded. "So instead of following the trail backwards from Porter, we follow it forwards from Tommy."

"Exactly," Raine confirmed.

"Who's dead," Sommers pointed out. "Just saying."

"But he left stuff behind," Raine said. "Everyone has stuff. We go through his belongings and see if it leads us to Porter or whoever paid him off."

OPHELIA HAD a spare key to Tommy's apartment, a necessity with a son with a drug problem. She needed to be able to get inside if he stopped answering her calls; he needed her to cosign the lease. The rent was paid through the end of the month, and Ophelia hadn't been able to bring herself to clean the place out yet.

Raine picked the key up from Ophelia and met Sommers at the apartment the next morning. It was 10:00 a.m. but felt like 6:00 p.m. A thick cloud cover dimmed the sun, and a light rain fell, pulling the scent of oil and dust from the pavement and bricks that surrounded them.

The apartment was a basement studio unit in an old brick building at the base of Queen Anne Hill. It had an exterior entry, several steps down from the parking lot around back, and only one small, dirty window to connect it with the outside world.

"This is depressing," Sommers opined.

"Probably just the weather," Raine suggested as he unlocked the door. "I'm sure it's delightful inside."

It was not. They swapped the smell of wet parking lot for the even more unpleasant scents of body odor and mold. And spoiled food. Definitely spoiled food.

"Yikes." Sommers covered her nose. "This is terrible. Who would live like this?"

In addition to the smell, the apartment was also visually despairing. A single futon with blankets half on the floor. Clothes strewn everywhere. Food wrappers and take-out boxes and mail covering the rest of the floor.

"A drug addict," Raine knew. "So much for him being clean."

"In more ways than one." Sommers nudged a dirty sock with her foot. "Now what? What are we looking for exactly?"

"I'm not sure," Raine admitted. "Something helpful."

Sommers laughed. "Like a confession from Porter?"

"I don't think Porter did anything," Raine answered. "It was somebody who needed Porter to be quiet. Look for something about that."

Sommers shook her head and looked around the tiny hovel. "Well, you did warn me it wouldn't be glamorous."

"You don't think you could flip this place?" Raine joked.

"I could flip anything," Sommers responded. "But it would take some work. And bleach. Lots of bleach."

Raine didn't disagree, but they weren't there to judge Tommy. They were there to avenge him, at least within the limits of the judicial system.

Raine expected to rifle through the drawers of a desk, but there was no desk. There wasn't even a table. Just that single futon. So he started there, pulling away the blankets and checking under the cushion.

Sommers circled the edges of the room, using her shoes to turn things over lest she have to touch anything with her hands.

Raine knew they couldn't both do that, and set out on a more systematic search of the one-room residence. He pulled everything two feet from the far wall, then made his way back toward the door, examining each item on the floor before discarding it behind him again.

Sommers mostly just tried to stay out of his way. "Finding anything?" she asked.

Raine shook his head. Used napkins. Used Kleenex. Used a lot of things. No used syringes, though. *Small mercies*, he thought. But he was careful not to stick his hand anywhere he couldn't see under.

He was beginning to lose hope when he came across a

small wad of cash. Several crumpled-up $20 bills. It was notable for two reasons. First, Tommy hadn't spent it immediately. Second, there was a small slip of paper at the center of the bundle.

"This might be something." He held it up for Sommers to see.

"What does it say?"

Raine frowned. "Just some letters and numbers. 124 EMW P32. Not sure what it means."

Sommers took the paper from Raine gingerly, between two fingers. "It's an address. 124 East Marginal Way, Pier 32."

Raine's eyebrows shot up. "Are you kidding me? How could you tell that?"

"I know Pier 32 is in the one-hundred-block of East Marginal Way South," Sommers answered. "I know every block of this city. Or at least the downtown core."

"And First Hill," Raine added with an admiring grin. "Do you know what's there?"

"Not off the top of my head," Sommers admitted. "But that's easy to figure out."

"And we already know one thing about it," Raine said, holding up the cash. "He made two hundred dollars for going there."

"We're going there too, I take it?" Sommers asked. "I bet we won't get two hundred dollars."

"No, but we might get something more valuable," Raine said. "Answers."

13

It was dusk before Raine and Sommers made their way to 124 East Marginal Way South. East because it was on the east side of the Duwamish River that emptied into Elliott Bay at the center of the city's working harbor; south because it was south of the city's commercial downtown. And Pier 32 because there were, or had been at least, thirty-one others wrapping around Elliott Bay. It wasn't the tourist waterfront anymore. It was the waterfront for sailors and longshoremen. And Axis Global Import-Export, the only business on Pier 32.

"It looks like a warehouse," Raine observed. "Definitely not a store."

The windowless building ran the length of the short pier, seemingly made of the same weathered wood as the dock itself. There was a single door at the far end, the one Raine and Sommers found themselves standing before, with a simple sign to the side of it displaying the name of the business. It was a nice logo, with a stylized globe behind gold lettering.

"Do you think they're still open?" Sommers asked. "They don't look open. But I'm not sure what open would look like for a business like this."

Raine checked the time. 5:37. Whether it was still open likely depended on how industrious the owners were. He imagined you needed to be pretty industrious to succeed in the import-export business.

"There's one way to find out," Raine answered. He reached out and turned the doorknob. It unlatched the door. "Yep, they're open."

He pulled the door all the way open and allowed Sommers to enter first, following close behind into the brightly lit room. He closed the dimming evening behind them.

The room was small and smelled of salt-soaked wood. There was a small desk with nothing on it and three mismatched chairs. Nothing on the walls and a single, closed door leading back toward the interior of the building they had just walked along. No one was there.

"Hello?" Raine called out. Maybe they weren't so industrious after all. Just forgetful and left the front door open.

"This is a bit of a surprise," Sommers commented with a shrug toward the bare desk. "I would have expected a receptionist at least."

"Well, it is after five," Raine allowed. "Maybe we can come back tomorrow. I'm just not sure if we should lock the door behind us."

The door to the back suddenly opened, and a man stepped through. "No need to lock that door, sir. This one locks quite well."

The man was very tall, with graying hair swept back from his narrow face. He wore a white linen shirt, the ends of the sleeves turned back once, khaki pants, and dark leather shoes. An expensive-looking watch weighed down his left wrist. His right bore an even more expensive-looking gold bracelet.

"Can I help you?" the man asked, with a slight accent Raine couldn't quite identify.

"I hope so," Raine answered. He didn't have an elaborate story made up to trick whomever they encountered into unwittingly divulging useful information. He barely had any information himself. "Do you happen to know someone named Tommy Wilson?"

"Do," not "did." He could hold back at least that much to start.

The man took a moment to think. Either to search his memory for the name, or decide whether to admit to knowing it. "I don't believe so. Should I?"

"I'm an attorney," Raine went ahead and admitted. "This is my investigator. We represent Tommy's family, and we have reason to believe he has a connection to this business."

The man frowned, which somehow made his handsome face even more appealing. "Is he missing?"

"He's dead," Sommers said. Obviously, she could tell Raine wasn't playing games. "We found the address for this business in his belongings. Along with a rather large amount of cash."

The man's frown shifted. "I can't explain that. Perhaps he was working for someone else."

"Like a delivery driver?" Sommers suggested.

One of the man's eyebrows rose. "I'm sure I don't know."

Sommers frowned at Raine. "I told you this was a waste of time. Let's just tell Detective Gillespie what we found and let the police handle it."

Raine stopped himself from squinting at Sommers in surprise. "Right. Detective Gillespie. He would probably be interested in all of this." He gestured vaguely around the undecorated space.

"I'm sure we don't need to involve the police," the man said, flashing a practiced smile. He pointed to the chairs pushed against the walls. "Let's the three of us sit down, and perhaps we can figure out why your Mr. Wilson had my address among his possessions."

Raine and Sommers agreed, and in a moment, they were all seated, facing each other in an awkward circle.

"Let us begin with introductions," the man said. "I am Armand Kasaybian. I am the proprietor here."

Sommers deferred to Raine with a small nod.

"Daniel Raine," he introduced himself. "I'm an attorney here in town."

Kasaybian nodded and turned his attention to Sommers.

"Rebecca Sommers," she said. "For today's purposes, I'm an investigator."

"Ah." Kasaybian nodded. "I feel like I've heard your name before, Ms. Sommers."

"Very likely," Sommers replied with a grin.

"But not yours, Mr. Raine," Kasaybian continued. "My apologies. I have not been in your city for very long yet."

"That's okay," Raine assured him. "No one wants to know an attorney until they need one."

"Well, then, let us hope I never need one." Kasaybian laughed. "But someone needed your services. This is what has brought you to my door. Tell me more. Tell me everything."

So Raine did. Not everything, of course. There was something disarming about the man, but Raine didn't trust Kasaybian yet; they had only just met. But Kasaybian hadn't given Raine a reason to distrust him either. Raine told him about Tommy's death. Ophelia's arrest. The criminal case. The civil case. Even Officer Porter's untimely death. But not the part about Officer Porter's extra funding sources or his extreme reaction to being found out. Then he repeated and expanded on their discovery in Tommy's apartment.

"And that's what brought us here," Raine concluded.

"Hmm." Kasaybian leaned back in his chair and pressed a hand tightly against his mouth in a very concerned expression. "That is all very interesting. Very interesting. But I'm afraid it has nothing to do with me."

"Well, the address does," Sommers responded.

"If that was even an address," Kasaybian countered. "It might be a computer password or safe combination for all we know."

Raine frowned. And there was the reason to distrust him. The scribble on Tommy's note certainly could have been one of those other things. But they all knew it wasn't.

Raine slapped his hands on his knees and stood up. "Welp, I guess that's what we came for. Sorry if we wasted your time, Mr. Kasaybian. Thanks for your hospitality."

Sommers followed suit, and Kasaybian stood as well. "I wish I could have been of more help, but it was nice to meet the both of you."

"Likewise," Raine returned. Then, to Sommers with a nod to the exit, "Ready?"

Sommers answered in the affirmative and took a step toward the door.

Then Kasaybian spoke up again. "Do you happen to have a business card? In case I learn something more and need to contact you."

Raine nodded and reached for his wallet. "What kind of lawyer would I be if I didn't always have a card on me?"

"I don't have any for this particular role," Sommers explained.

Raine extracted a business card from his wallet and handed it to Kasaybian. "Here you go."

"J. Daniel Raine, Attorney at Law," Kasaybian read aloud. "What does the *J* stand for? Justice?"

Raine smiled. "It does now. I like that."

Once they were outside and off the pier again, Sommers looked up at Raine. "He didn't win you over with that '*J* is for justice' thing, did he?"

Raine laughed. "Oh, I'm definitely going to be using that. But no. He may not have lied to us, but he didn't tell us the truth either."

"So what next?" Sommers asked.

Raine considered what they had learned, what they hadn't, and, most importantly, his schedule for the next several days. He looked north to the skyline, the windows of its buildings lit up against the darkening sky. "Next, I have to act like a lawyer again."

14

Two weeks later came the most important deposition of the entire civil case: Dr. Peter Nieuwendyk, medical examiner. Assistant medical examiner, actually. He wasn't the boss. His job wasn't supervising personnel and managing budgets. It was carving up bodies and writing up reports. He knew his stuff. Raine needed to know it too, even if only to be able to explain to the jury why they shouldn't believe it.

The deposition was scheduled to take place at Raine's office this time. Nieuwendyk was a professional. He didn't need to feel protected by the prosecutor's office. He showed up on time, as did Pierce and the court reporter. It was a simple matter of swearing in the doctor and they were off to the races.

"Please state your full name for the record." Raine started the deposition with the same first question.

"Peter James Nieuwendyk," the doctor answered. Then he provided his date of birth, business address, and complete educational and work history. Medical school.

General residency. Specialized residency in pathology. Three years with the Snohomish County Medical Examiner's Office. Twenty-one more with the King County ME. Too many autopsies to count. "Thousands," he assured him.

Raine had no doubt it was true. He wasn't going to convince a jury that Nieuwendyk wasn't qualified. He was going to have to convince them that on this one case, he'd made a mistake.

"Let's talk about the autopsy of Thomas Wilson." Raine narrowed the scope of the interview. "Do you have a copy of your autopsy report with you?"

He did, of course. So did Raine. Pierce, as well. They could all follow along.

"Let's get right to it, then," Raine said. "If you could turn to page twelve of your report. You indicate there your conclusion as to the cause of death. You seem to say that Mr. Wilson died due to the drugs in his system, but the toxicology report showed only trace levels of opiates and amphetamines. How could he have died of a drug overdose if the levels were barely enough to even make a person high?"

"A fair question," Nieuwendyk allowed, "but one that misstates my conclusions. I didn't say that Mr. Wilson died of a drug overdose. I said I couldn't determine an exact cause of death. I opined that he might have died of organ failure secondary to drug use."

"Right, organ failure." Raine nodded. "He was twenty-two. Wouldn't it be extremely unusual for someone in his twenties to suffer organ failure?"

"Yes, it would," Nieuwendyk agreed. "That's why I believe it was secondary to the drug use."

"And which organs, exactly?" Raine pressed. "All of them?"

"Enough of them to kill him," was the answer.

"Excuse me, Doctor"—Raine shook his head—"but that seems like a guess."

"In a way, it is," Nieuwendyk admitted.

Raine looked over to Pierce. "Jury's not going to like that, Jackson. Not one bit."

Pierce just smiled back confidently. "I guess we'll see."

Raine turned back to Nieuwendyk. "So you just guess how someone died? That doesn't seem very scientific. Why can't I guess too? I think the cops did it. There. Are we both right?"

"Every case is different," the doctor protested with a slight sigh. "I'm sure it's the same in your work. Some cases are easy. A gunshot wound to the head, say. Others are more difficult. This case was a bit of a process of elimination. An otherwise healthy young man died. That's where I started. Then I worked backward to try to determine how. There were no signs of trauma on the body. No gunshot wounds or wounds from sharp force or blunt force trauma. That means no one shot him or stabbed him or beat him with a club."

"I know what sharp and blunt force trauma mean, Doctor," Raine replied.

"All right. Well, then you also know that if it's not an external force that caused the death, it must logically have been an internal force. It could have been natural causes, but he was far too young to die from that absent some major medical issue of which I'm unaware and evidence of which I didn't observe. There were no cancerous tumors, for example. In fact, all of his organs were perfectly healthy, with the exception of some slight damage to his lungs from smoking, but nothing that would have caused death. There being no external forces and no natural causes, that leaves just toxins, and he did have toxins in his body, in the form of the drugs he had ingested."

"Drugs that weren't at a sufficient level to cause an overdose," Raine reminded him. "In fact, these are all very low levels, almost residual from the previous day."

"Well, you have to remember," Nieuwendyk defended, "those results indicate what was in his blood at the time the blood was taken out of the body, not at the time of death. Although we endeavor to collect blood samples as quickly as possible, there will be some degradation of the drugs from the decomposition of the body."

"What drugs do you test for?" Raine asked.

"There's a standard array of tests for the most common street drugs," Nieuwendyk explained.

"Like what?" Raine pressed.

"Oh, you know, the usual suspects," Nieuwendyk answered. "Cocaine, opiates, cannabis."

"Are there any things they don't automatically test for?" Raine asked.

"Of course," Nieuwendyk confirmed.

"Like what?" Raine followed up.

Nieuwendyk shrugged. "A million things. Caffeine. Creatine. Ginseng. We only test for things that we know from experience can cause damage or death."

"What about some new street drug you'd never heard of?" Raine suggested.

"Well, I'm not sure..." Nieuwendyk hesitated. "If there were some new, experimental drug that we'd never heard of, I suppose we wouldn't know to test for it."

"Experimental?" Raine didn't hate that. "Do you think

the government injected him with an experimental drug? There's precedent for that, you know."

Nieuwendyk frowned. "That's not what I said."

"Kinda sounds like what you said to me." Raine looked again to Pierce. "What do you think, Jackson?"

"I think you're fishing," Pierce replied. "And you're not catching anything. How much more do you have? We all have other things to do, I'm sure."

"No, I'm good," Raine answered. "I blocked off the whole day for this."

Nieuwendyk's shoulders drooped. "I'm sure I don't have a day's worth of material to share with you, counselor. Your client was otherwise healthy, but he died anyway, and the only explanation I can offer is that he had drugs in his system that caused one or more vital systems to fail. That's it."

"He's not my client," Raine corrected. "His mother is."

"In more ways than one," Pierce quipped. "Literally."

Nieuwendyk frowned at the prosecutor. "I don't understand."

"In addition to losing her son to the negligence of the government," Raine explained, "that same government is also charging Tommy's mother with crimes for daring to speak publicly about his death."

Nieuwendyk's eyebrows knitted together. "That doesn't seem fair."

And suddenly Raine didn't hate the doctor after all. "It isn't." He pointed at Pierce. "Tell that guy."

But Pierce raised his hands. "Whoa. Different division. I'm a civil guy. I don't handle criminal cases."

Raine shook his head. "You know what? I think I have enough here. The good doctor will tell the jury he doesn't know why Tommy died, but he has a guess. An educated guess, but still a guess. What isn't a guess is that it happened while he was in the custody of the county jail. It's also not a guess that when his mother complained about it, she was arrested and railroaded to shut her up. I'm happy to take that to a jury. We can let them decide how much to pay my client for what your client has put her through."

Pierce took a moment to digest Raine's outburst. "So we can let Dr. Nieuwendyk go? Maybe you and I could take a moment then to talk about the case. I don't completely agree with your assessment."

"I wouldn't expect you to," Raine answered. "But yes. Fine. Dr. Nieuwendyk can go. I'll see you at the trial, Doctor, when you're on the witness stand, trying to explain to the jury why you don't know how to do your one job."

Dr. Nieuwendyk offered a pained smile. "I'll be sure to prepare my testimony accordingly. Nice to meet you, Mr. Raine." He stood up to take his leave. "Good to see you again, Mr. Pierce."

Raine escorted Nieuwendyk to the exit, then returned to the conference room to negotiate with Pierce. Maybe his offer had gone up. Twenty thousand and a dismissal of the criminal charges would at least cover his expenses.

"My offer has gone down." Pierce opened the negotiations. "I can offer you five thousand to go away. Then you handle the criminal case however you see fit."

"Five thousand and go to trial on felony charges?" Raine replied. "That's insulting."

Pierce shrugged. "My case is stronger than it was the last time we talked."

"How so?" Raine questioned. "Your doc can't say why my

client's son died. And they burned the body before we could have our own expert look at it."

"That last part is your fault, from what I hear." Pierce grinned. "Called away before you could demand the body be preserved."

Raine felt a rush of guilt shoot up the back of his neck.

"And I believe you also get credit for my case getting stronger," Pierce continued.

"How so?" Raine asked.

"Recall our last depositions," Pierce answered, "when you pointed out that my two corrections officers had differing stories. Well, now that's no longer a problem for me. Officer Porter is no longer available as a witness. And I hear I have you to thank for that as well."

"Not me," Raine assured him. "But someone wanted to silence him. And I suspect they're a lot closer to you than they are to me."

15

The following week, Raine shifted back to the criminal case for what was called the "omnibus hearing." Raine told clients that "omnibus" was Latin for "everything," and it was the hearing where the judge made sure everything was ready for trial. He'd never actually bothered to look up the translation to see if he was right about the word, but he was definitely right about the hearing. He'd done enough of them to know. And to know not to be late.

For her part, Ophelia knew to listen to her lawyer and not be late. The hearing was at 1:00 p.m. in Judge Taylor's courtroom on the seventh floor. They met at 12:30 in a client meeting room outside the law library on the first floor.

"I'm sorry to admit it, Mr. Raine," Ophelia started, "but I'm starting to get a little bit scared. What if all this doesn't turn out like it should?"

Raine nodded. This was the first time Ophelia Wilson was experiencing the particular set of emotions associated with realizing that, regardless of truth, justice, and the

American way, you might get convicted of a crime you didn't commit and go to prison. Some people might even argue that was the American way. But it wasn't supposed to be. And Raine had had this conversation more times than he could count. His reply was at the ready.

"It's good that you're scared," he answered. "You should be. It means you're paying attention. You know what's at stake."

"Everything," Ophelia half whispered.

"Exactly," Raine agreed with what was to him hyperbole, but to her, reality.

"What if we lose?" she pressed. "I can't go to prison, Mr. Raine."

"I know." Raine tried to soothe her, but his ethical rules got in the way. "I wish I could promise that won't happen, but I can never promise what a jury will do. All I can promise is to do my best and give the jury what they need to do the right thing."

Ophelia looked down at her interlocked hands and absorbed his answer in silence for several moments. She looked up again. "Maybe we should settle the cases. Maybe I should take a plea bargain. Maybe I should dismiss the case about Tommy."

Raine frowned, only slightly on the outside; deeper, within. "Ultimately, those are your decisions. I can advise you against it, but you have to make the final decision."

"What was the offer again?" Ophelia asked.

"The offer was to dismiss the civil case completely," Raine reminded her, "and plead guilty to some misdemeanors."

"Is that still on the table?" Ophelia asked.

Raine shook his head. "No. The latest offer is five thousand to make the civil case go away and take our chances on the criminal case. They'd probably let you plead to the felonies and dismiss the misdemeanors."

"Is that a good result?"

"That is a terrible result," Raine answered. "It's about the same as we would get if we went to trial on both cases and lost them both. Five thousand is as close to zero as a case like this gets. And if you go down on the felonies, the misdemeanors won't matter anyway."

"So what do we do?" Ophelia's eyes were welling up with fear and helplessness.

"We fight," Raine answered. "And, God willing, we win. We hold them responsible for what they did to Tommy and what they did to you. It won't bring Tommy back, but it will teach them a lesson."

Ophelia seemed unconvinced.

"And maybe," Raine added, "the next Ophelia Wilson won't lose her son to the negligence of the county jail and won't be arrested for daring to speak out."

Ophelia's eyes brightened at that.

"This case is bigger than just you and Tommy," Raine told her. "Every case is bigger than just the litigants. This is about making them pay for what they did, what they're doing. But it's also to make sure they damn well never do it again."

Those wet, brightening eyes narrowed. "You're right, Mr. Raine."

Of course I am, Raine thought. *This is what I do.* "Then let's show them we're right. Or scare the hell out of them trying."

Ophelia reached out and grabbed Raine's hands. "Thank you, Mr. Raine."

Raine extracted his hands and placed them on top of his client's. "We have a lot of work ahead of us still. Don't thank me just yet. Help me."

"Anything," Ophelia agreed. "Just tell me what to do."

"For today, I just need you to sit next to me and look confident," Raine instructed. "I want them to wonder why you aren't nervous. I want them to wonder why they should be."

"I can do that," Ophelia assured him.

"I know." Raine smiled. "Now, let's go upstairs and tell the judge we're ready for trial."

JUDGE LUCAS TAYLOR was one of the more ambitious judges on the King County bench. Raine had first encountered him when he was a municipal prosecutor for one of the more remote suburbs of Seattle. From there, he got himself appointed as that town's judge, for a municipal court that only convened once a month and then almost exclusively for parking tickets and traffic infractions.

Taylor used that position to run as a "judge" for the far larger Seattle Municipal Court. Still a muni court. Still parking tickets and traffic infractions, but also criminal misdemeanors. And connections. And donors. He shook hands and patted backs and made friends with all of the other, higher judges in the county. Eventually one of those judges retired from the County Superior Court and told Taylor first. Taylor filed for the position, published his endorsements and campaign account balance, and no one dared file against him.

Raine wondered when Taylor would make a move for the

Court of Appeals, but until then he was, despite or perhaps because of his naked ambition, a pretty good judge. Raine would never begrudge anyone for pursuing their goals. But he would always try to use it to the advantage of his client.

First and foremost, that meant showing respect for the position and the man. That meant being early. Nothing angered a judge more than taking the bench and seeing an empty chair where a lawyer was supposed to be. Clients, especially criminal defendants, were late or completely absent all of the time. There were court rules in place for precisely that eventuality. But lawyers could, should, and would always be in the courtroom before the judge emerged from their chambers to a hearty call of the bailiff.

"All rise! The King County Superior Court is now in session, the Honorable Lucas Taylor presiding!"

Raine and Ophelia stood from their seats at the defendant's table. Catherine Tennet stood as well, from her spot next to them at the plaintiff's table. The rest of the courtroom was empty save the bailiff and the court reporter.

Some of the judges set a dozen omnibus hearings all for the same time at the start of the calendar and let the lawyers fight out who would go first. Judge Taylor set the same dozen cases for one afternoon, but one after another, fifteen minutes apart. Four per hour, plus a fifteen-minute break for his staff, and they would finish at 4:15, well before the courtrooms filled with still-wrangling prosecutors and defense attorneys, some of whom wouldn't bother showing up at 1:00 if they weren't going to be heard first anyway.

"Are the parties ready on the matter of *The State of Washington versus*"—Judge Taylor glanced down at the paper docket before him—"*Ophelia Wilson?*"

"The State is ready, Your Honor." Tennet addressed the Court first.

The prosecutor always went first. In theory, that was so the defense would have the advantage of knowing what the prosecution might say before having to respond. In practice, because most prosecutors acted like they were running the courtroom rather than the judge.

"The defense is ready as well, Your Honor," Raine answered in turn.

"Good." Taylor nodded with satisfaction. He was a thin, wiry man, with shortly cropped hair over his ears and a shiny bald head, where he routinely perched his reading glasses. "Then let us begin. Trial is scheduled to begin in two weeks, is that correct?"

"Two weeks from Monday," Tennet clarified. "Yes, Your Honor."

"Does either side anticipate requesting a continuance of that trial date?" Judge Taylor asked next.

The judge had a checklist. It would take fourteen minutes to complete, Raine knew.

"No, Your Honor," Tennet answered. She was still standing.

Raine was standing too. Lawyers were always supposed to stand when addressing a judge. They let it slide in some of the muni courts, but not in Superior Court. Not in Judge Taylor's court.

Raine did motion for Ophelia to sit down. She wasn't going to be doing any talking that day. Not any day until the day she took the stand in her own defense at the end of the jury trial they were in the process of confirming. "No, Your Honor," he answered the judge's question.

"Good," Taylor repeated. "How long does each side expect the trial to last?"

Tennet thought for a moment. "Four to five days, Your Honor."

Raine scoffed, but not so loudly that the judge heard him.

"Do you agree, Mr. Raine?" Judge Taylor asked.

"I do not, Your Honor," Raine answered. "I expect to take at least twice that long."

Taylor frowned. He glanced again at the papers in front of him. "For an assault three case?"

"Assault in third degree, intimidation of a public servant, disorderly conduct, criminal trespass in the second degree, and two other piled-on charges that escape me at the moment."

There was respect for the judge, but there was also advocacy for the client. It was important for the respect to flow both ways, and few judges respected a lawyer who didn't show a little life and advocate for their client.

When Judge Taylor raised an eyebrow at his answer, Raine added, "I expect to conduct a vigorous and lengthy cross-examination of each and every one of the State's witnesses."

"I have no doubt," Judge Taylor answered with a slight grin. He turned to Tennet. "How many of those witnesses does the State expect to call?"

Tennet took a moment before speaking. "Nine, Your Honor."

Taylor nodded. "So more than four days. Who are these witnesses, and what will they be testifying to?"

"Six of them are the officers who were involved in the arrest of the defendant," Tennet answered.

Taylor's eyebrows rose again, both of them. And he glanced down at the middle-aged woman sitting quietly at the defendant's table. "It took six officers to arrest the defendant?"

"Six officers were involved, Your Honor," Tennet responded. "Not all of them laid hands on the defendant."

Because one of them was laying hands on me, Raine thought, but he kept the thought to himself.

"Okay. Who else?" Taylor asked.

"Well, then there's the medical examiner," Tennet continued.

"Medical examiner?" Taylor interrupted. "Why is a medical examiner testifying in an assault trial? I assume if one of the officers had died, this would be a murder trial. What am I missing?"

Raine turned to watch Tennet squirm as she tried to explain. He allowed himself a small, yet professional smile.

"The defendant was arrested after failing to disperse outside the King County Jail, Your Honor," Tennet said. "She was protesting because her son had recently died while in custody, and she blamed the jail."

Taylor leaned back in his chair and twisted his mouth into a thoughtful knot. "So the medical examiner will say it wasn't the jail's fault?"

"Yes," Tennet answered.

"No," Raine interjected. "Not after I'm done with him."

Judge Taylor leaned forward again. "Not to impugn your skills at cross-examination, Mr. Raine, but now is not the time to assert what might or might not be said at trial."

"I'm asserting what Dr. Nieuwendyk already said at his deposition," Raine explained. "He doesn't actually know how my client died. Or at least that's what he claims now that she's suing the county for wrongful death."

Taylor nodded slowly and sighed audibly. "I see. There is a concurrent civil case proceeding as well, is that correct?"

"Yes, Your Honor," Raine confirmed.

"We will be moving to exclude any specifics of that case from the trial, Your Honor," Tennet announced, "other than to show that the defendant has a motive to lie in the event she elects to take the stand."

"What motive is that, Ms. Tennet?" Judge Taylor asked.

"Money, Your Honor," Tennet answered. "She is suing for money, and a conviction in this case will surely make it more difficult to win that case."

Taylor frowned. "I'm not so sure of that," he opined aloud. "So, you want to tell the jury that she's suing the county because they caused her son's death, but then have the medical examiner tell the jury that it wasn't the jail's fault. Is that accurate?"

"Yes, Your Honor," Tennet agreed.

The judge looked again to the defense table. "What do you think about that, Mr. Raine?"

"I think that would be an exceptionally unfair cherry-picking of the relevant facts," Raine answered. "I think it shows how weak the State's case really is. They don't want the jury to think Ms. Wilson may have had a point. They're afraid of what a jury will do if they hear she was right to try to hold the jail accountable. They know the jury will see through this sham of a case for what it really is: a vindictive prosecution designed to punish a citizen for exercising her constitutional rights to freedom of speech, peaceable assembly, and petition for redress of grievances."

"That seems like that might also be a bridge too far, Mr.

Raine." Judge Taylor raised a hand at him. "I'm sure we can craft a way of trying this case without connecting it to a pending civil case."

"The prosecution has connected them, Your Honor," Raine protested. "Every offer we have received on this case has been conditioned on some action in the civil case as well."

Judge Taylor frowned at Tennet. "Is that true?"

"The cases are related factually, Your Honor," Tennet defended. "It's not that the offers were necessarily contingent on each other, but it's only natural that my office, the criminal and civil sides, would make offers on both cases."

"Simultaneously?" Taylor demanded.

"Well, yes," Tennet admitted. "But to be fair, Your Honor, Mr. Raine represents the defendant on both cases. It would be silly not to save time and communicate offers together."

Taylor's frown deepened, but he turned to Raine. "Is that how you would characterize it, Mr. Raine? Simultaneous but separate?"

"That is not how I would characterize it, Your Honor," Raine answered.

Taylor seemed to expect that answer. "So, what are you going to do about it?"

Raine reached into his briefcase and extracted a set of documents. "I am going to file a motion to dismiss for vindictive prosecution, Your Honor. And I am going to ask that it be heard prior to the trial."

"We only have two weeks until trial!" Tennet protested even as Raine handed a copy of the motion to her.

He stepped forward and handed the original to the bailiff. "Two weeks from Monday. And the court rules only require one week's notice. There is plenty of time to hear this motion. And if I win, we won't even need a trial."

Judge Taylor accepted the motion from his bailiff and perused it even as Tennet sputtered through a series of "But, Your Honors."

"This appears to be in order," Taylor announced. "And Mr. Raine is correct. He only needs to give you a week's notice. I'm going to schedule this for a hearing one week from Monday. And I'm going to schedule it in my courtroom. I will keep this case for trial."

Raine smiled. That was the play. He could have filed the motion with the clerk of the court and delivered a copy to Tennet's office. But he wanted Taylor to know about it because he wanted Taylor to decide it. An ambitious judge is a careful judge. Raine was going to give him a chance to stand up for an average citizen against overreach by the police and prosecution. That might not get him points with every voter, but it might make him some friends with the more liberal judges on the Court of Appeals.

Tennet dropped her head and sighed. Which was all she had time to do anyway. Their fifteen minutes was up.

"We can conclude the omnibus hearing after the hearing on Mr. Raine's motion to dismiss," Judge Taylor declared, "if we still need to, that is."

Raine liked that addition.

"We are ready for the next case," Judge Taylor went on. "This matter is adjourned until nine a.m. one week from Monday." He banged his gavel.

Raine and Ophelia had to scramble to get out of the way of the next defense attorney and defendant as Judge Taylor began reading the name of the next case.

Raine gathered up his things, and they quickly exited

into the hallway for a post-court huddle. Mostly just Raine asking Ophelia if she understood what had happened, Ophelia saying not really, and Raine telling her the hearing went well, and they would meet again before the next hearing, a week from Monday.

Raine figured that would end his time at the courthouse, but as he finished parting ways with Ophelia, Tennet walked up to him and asked, "Can we talk for a minute, Mr. Raine?"

"Dan," Raine insisted. "And sure. Go ahead. Talk."

Tennet frowned and glanced around. "Not here. Can you come to my office? It's here in the courthouse."

"I know it is," Raine replied. "One more institutional advantage for the prosecution."

Tennet shrugged and shook her head. "Whatever. I want to talk to you about this motion."

"I'm sure you do," Raine almost gloated.

"But not here," Tennet repeated. "I don't need this to be overheard."

"You don't need what to be overheard?" Raine asked.

"What I'm going to tell you about this case," Tennet answered. "And what you need to do to win."

16

The criminal division of the King County Prosecutor's Office was located on the fifth floor of the courthouse. Raine followed Tennet down the two flights of stairs, through the lobby, and to her personal office tucked away amid a maze of windowless hallways.

"Nice office," Raine said anyway as he stepped inside.

They both knew he was lying. It was cramped, barely large enough for her desk let alone the one guest chair positioned awkwardly to one side. She had a window, but the view was just the next building over. She hadn't worked her way up to a water view yet.

Tennet closed the door and stepped awkwardly around the guest chair to get to her own seat. "Good enough," she defended as she sat down at her desk. "It's not like I have to impress clients."

"Well, that's good," Raine said. "So, shall we cut to the chase? I have a hearing to prepare for."

Tennet sighed. "Look, I get it," she started.

Raine doubted that very much. She just admitted she

didn't have clients—just some amorphous concept of "the people" and "justice," which, coincidentally, could just happen to line up with whatever her personal thoughts and feelings were. And if she lost, no one was going to prison. But Raine let her continue without interruption.

"You think your client got a bad rap," Tennet went on. "You think the cops treated her unfairly. They should have just let her yell and cry and get it out of her system. You think they could have handled it differently, and then neither of us would be here right now."

"I think a lot of that, yes," Raine agreed, "and more."

"So, look, here's the thing." Tennet leaned forward. "I don't actually care about this case. Not any more than any of the other twenty or thirty I have in my file cabinet right now. But I have a job to do. Like I said, I don't have clients, but I have a boss. And my boss will be super pissed at me if this case gets dismissed because of a finding of vindictive prosecution."

"Ah." Raine thought he knew where Tennet was going, but also knew to let her lead the way.

"That's a big freaking deal," Tennet continued. "Like, bar complaint big. Judges never find it, but Taylor might. That guy is always thinking of the next big play, and it doesn't get much bigger than issuing a ruling of a vindictive prosecution. Do you know how rare those are?"

"I do, in fact," Raine answered. "I wrote a brief on it, remember?"

"Right, right." Tennet waved her hand at him. "Fine. Well, however few there have been, I don't want to be the one who added one to the pile. Do you know what that will do to my reputation? Not just here, but everywhere in the state? I won't be able to go to a conference without people whispering behind my back."

"This must be really difficult for you," Raine said. "Have you met my client yet? The one you're trying to put in prison?"

Tennet shook her head. "I don't care if your client goes to prison or not."

"Well, that's kind of my point," Raine interjected. "I would like you to care, and I would like you to not do it. Hence, my motion."

"What I mean is"—Tennet sighed again—"this is just another case for me, and every now and again, cases go south. Victims don't cooperate. Witnesses disappear. Lab results don't say what you want them to say. There are a hundred reasons a case might fall apart. Give me one of those instead."

Raine cocked his head at her. "What?"

"Give me a different reason to dump this case," Tennet expanded. "Something other than vindictive prosecution."

"Just dismiss it!" Raine threw his hands up. "You have the power to do that. Any time. Go upstairs right now and have Taylor sign off on a dismissal order."

"I can't do it for no reason," Tennet complained. "Like I said, I have a boss. And he has a boss. And so does she. And there are six cops and a bunch of other law enforcement types watching this case very closely. They will want to know why I dismissed a case where they are the victims."

"Tell them she's innocent," Raine suggested.

But Tennet shook her head. "They won't accept that. They arrested her because they thought she was guilty."

"They arrested her because she was daring to speak up about them," Raine countered.

"Agree to disagree." Tennet waved her hand at Raine again. "We're getting off topic."

"This seems very on topic," Raine argued.

Tennet shook her head again. "No, you're missing my point. I'm telling you what you need to do to get this case dismissed, if you can do it before the hearing on your motion for vindictive prosecution. Get me something. Something real. Something that shows your client had a legitimate reason to be upset with how her son died. Something that shows actual liability on behalf of the county. Get me that, and I can justify dismissing the case because no jury would convict her."

It was Raine's turn to sigh. Did she think he hadn't been looking for exactly that sort of evidence?

"Just throw the hearing on vindictive prosecution," he suggested. "Let Taylor dismiss it."

"Are you not listening?" Tennet ran her hands through her hair. "I cannot lose that motion. It will kill my career, and I will never get out of this closet of an office. If you get me something good, something I can paper my file with, then I will dismiss the charges prior to the hearing. But if you don't, and I have to do that hearing, then I will do everything in my power to win it. And I will win it."

Raine frowned. She probably would. He had done the research. There had only been two successful motions to dismiss for vindictiveness in the last fifty years, and both of those had far more egregious facts than he had. Every prosecution was vindictive in a way. That's what prosecution was: punishing people for what they did. There was a distinction between vindictive and vindicating. Odds were, he was going to lose that hearing. But Tennet was so scared of going down with the ship, she was throwing him a lifeline. He'd be a fool not to reach for it.

"Okay, I'll get you something," he promised.

"Something good," Tennet cautioned.

"Something good," Raine agreed, "and then you'll dismiss the case. Deal?"

"Deal," Tennet confirmed. "I just hope you can meet your end of it."

Raine hoped so too.

17

There were three women in Raine's life who might offer insight on what type of evidence Tennet would want to dismiss the case. One because she knew the case. One because she knew the law. And one because she knew Raine. He spoke to each in turn, but in the opposite order.

"Jordan! Jason! Your father is here!" Natalie shouted into the house after opening the door to find Raine standing on the porch. "And he's early," she added, just for him to hear.

"Yeah, sorry about that," Raine apologized. "I was hoping you might have a minute to talk about something."

Natalie hesitated. "Dan, we've talked about everything too many times already. There's nothing more to talk about. There's no more 'us' to talk about."

Raine took a moment to push down the feelings Natalie had unexpectedly stirred back up inside him. "Um, no. Not about us. Us is over. I get that. You made that abundantly clear when you filed for divorce, and a judge signed an order to that effect."

Natalie narrowed her eyes slightly. "Then what do you want to talk about? Is it the boys? Jason?"

Raine had to smile that they both knew if there was a problem with one of the boys, it was probably with Jason. There was still plenty of "us" between them.

"No, not the boys either," he assured her. "It's about one of my cases."

Natalie's head dropped to one side. "You want to talk to me about one of your cases?"

"Well, yes," Raine confirmed. "I thought maybe—"

"You don't get to talk to me about your work anymore, Dan," Natalie chided. "That's what being divorced means. We don't get to tell each other what to do, and we don't have to listen to each other's problems."

"I'm not asking you because you're my wife," Raine defended. "Or ex-wife. Or whatever. I'm asking you because you're smart."

Natalie took a beat. Then she shook her head, but smiled. "You're a lawyer all right. You always have an angle. You always have some way to make people answer your questions. Threats, tricks, flattery. You know what? Fine. I'll answer your stupid question. How can *I* help *you* with *your* case, Dan?"

"I think sometimes I grasp at straws because I don't want to face the fact that my hands are empty," Raine said. "I've got a case where if I grasp at a straw and I actually get it, I might be able to get the case dismissed. But I'm afraid there's no straw and I'm going to be left empty-handed. I think maybe I do that. I think maybe I did that a lot with you. With us."

Natalie listened patiently while Raine muddled through his vague question that turned out to not even be a question. She started to reach up to touch his face, but stopped herself. That was probably a good thing.

"You're a good man, Dan," she said. "You love your work, and you're good at it. Part of the reason you're good at it is that you take chances. I couldn't keep watching you do that with me and the boys. But you should keep doing it for your clients."

Raine smiled at the answer. A bittersweet smile, but a smile nonetheless.

Then the kids interrupted. Like they always did.

"Hey, Dad. What's for dinner?" Jordan was first out the door. "I want pizza."

"You always want pizza," Jason complained from a few steps behind. "I want Mexican."

Raine and Natalie met each other's eyes long enough to know to let go again.

"I was thinking I would cook tonight," Raine said, turning his attention to his boys.

"Wow, no." Jason made a retching noise. "I'd rather have pizza."

"Yay! Pizza!" Jordan called out from the car. "Meat supreme! And breadsticks!"

Raine turned back to the front door of the home he used to live in, and the woman he used to share it with. "Thanks, Nat."

"Whatever, Dan." Natalie shrugged off their conversation. "Go get the boys some pizza."

RAINE DEVOTED his weekend to spending time with his kids. After that, he made a point to spend time with his girlfriend. Their schedules had finally lined up to redo that dinner at Arturo's.

"Vindictive prosecution, huh?" Sawyer nodded approvingly over her drink. A blueberry cosmo or some such. "That's awesome. I've never heard of that before."

"That's because it's pretty much impossible to prove," Raine admitted. He had ordered his usual, an old-fashioned. But Sawyer's drink looked pretty good. He might try one of those on their next round.

"What do you have to show?" Sawyer asked. "I mean, aren't all prosecutors vindictive? That's, like, part of the job description, I think."

"You joke, but that's actually part of the problem," Raine answered. "It's not enough to show that the prosecutor filed the case in order to punish the defendant. Like you said, that's basically their job. You have to show that the only reason they did it was to punish the defendant for exercising a constitutional right."

"The only reason?" Sawyer raised an index finger. "That 'only' is pretty important."

"Exactly." Raine nodded. "Basically I would need to show that the only reason the case was filed was to punish her for exercising her constitutional right to protest the death of her son."

Sawyer stuck out a thoughtful lip. It was painted bright red, to match her off-the-shoulder dress and platform heels. "Well, you might be able to do that. She was exercising her right to free speech and all that."

Raine nodded again. "That's why the prosecutor is scared."

Sawyer smiled broadly. "I love it when the prosecutor is scared."

"Me too," Raine agreed. "But she's not going to concede the motion. If anything, she's going to fight like hell to win it because she's so scared of being the prosecutor who lost that motion."

"Makes sense." Sawyer took another sip of her drink. "It could be hard to live that down."

"So my question is this." Raine leaned forward and tipped his glass toward his companion. "Do I try to find this other reason to dismiss what she wants, or just double down on the vindictiveness motion and do everything I can to win that?"

Sawyer squinted at him. "Well, duh. You do both, obviously."

"Both?" Raine questioned. He leaned back again.

"You do everything, all the time, as many times as you need to," Sawyer answered. "That's the first rule of being a criminal defense attorney."

"I'm not sure that's a rule, actually," Raine critiqued. "Or if it is, it's, like, three rules."

"You know what I mean." Sawyer pointed at him with a grin. "Why are you even asking? Do both. Do more than both. Find her what she wants and get the case dismissed. Win the vindictiveness motion and get the case dismissed. Win the trial and get the case dismissed."

"If I win the trial, it's an acquittal, not a dismissal," Raine pointed out, to Sawyer's obvious annoyance. "But I get your point."

"Especially because you're probably going to lose the

vindictiveness motion," Sawyer continued. She picked up her phone.

"You think so?" Raine asked.

"Maybe," Sawyer answered. "Let's see. I'm pulling up your brief right now from the court website."

"You're going to read my brief to conclude that I'm going to lose?" Raine questioned.

"If your brief doesn't convince me," Sawyer explained, "it's not going to convince Judge Taylor."

Raine supposed that was true. He leaned back and scanned the restaurant while his date read his latest legal writing sample. It was pretty lively for a Tuesday. Remembering the day of the week reminded him that he had less than a week to get Tennet something, and he still had nothing. That was part of why he was hoping Sawyer might tell him to forget the uncertain something and focus on the definitely scheduled motion hearing.

"Yeah, you're going to lose," Sawyer finally said, looking up from her phone. "The case law on this is bad. The courts don't want to get involved in this kind of stuff if they don't absolutely have to. If there's any argument that the charges have merit, you lose. And these charges have merit. Minimal merit, but not zero merit."

"She didn't assault any of the officers," Raine insisted.

"Okay, but did she arguably disturb the peace, whatever the hell that means?" Sawyer challenged. "And if she did, did she refuse to leave the plaza after being told to do so for disturbing the peace? If so, that's trespassing."

Raine frowned, but didn't have a strong reply. It was one thing to argue to a jury that the facts didn't rise to proof beyond a reasonable doubt. It was another thing to convince a judge the facts didn't rise to any level at all.

"Taylor wants to get on the Court of Appeals, right?" Sawyer continued. "So he's not going to go out on a limb and dismiss a case he knows will immediately be appealed to that same Court of Appeals. Not unless his ruling is ironclad and airtight. And it wouldn't be, not on these facts. The last thing he wants is to be reversed by the very court he wants to be on. You think your prosecutor couldn't live down losing that motion. Taylor couldn't live down granting it and having the Court of Appeals tell him he's wrong."

"A good lawyer knows the law," Raine quoted the saying about lawyers, "but a great lawyer knows the judge."

Sawyer raised her glass to herself. "I am a great lawyer."

Raine raised his to her as well. "Yes, you are."

HIS LAST MEETING was with his partner in crime, so to speak, Rebecca Sommers. Although, if the course of action he needed to take did actually include committing a crime, he was inclined not to bring Sommers into it. He was a low-rent solo practitioner. If he went to jail, he could hand out business cards. Sommers was a high-rent real estate agent. If she went to jail, she could lose everything: her reputation, her license, her entire way of life.

Hopefully, they could think of something that wasn't criminal.

"Break into that warehouse," was Sommers's first suggestion. "Axis of Evil Import-Export, or whatever."

"Axis Global Import-Export." Raine had looked it up again before their meeting. Great minds think alike.

After dinner at a fancy Italian restaurant with Sawyer, lunch the next day with Sommers was at a simple Vietnamese sandwich shop in the International District, just a couple of blocks from Raine's office. The perfect place for bánh mì sandwiches and criminal conspiracies.

"Why them?" Raine asked. He thought he knew. He wanted to see if he was right.

"Well, the way I figure it"—Sommers leaned back and rubbed her chin thoughtfully—"we know that Armand guy was lying. Those numbers and letters on that scrap of paper from Tommy's apartment were definitely an address, and his address. He knew that, too. You could tell."

Raine nodded. He had the same impression.

"So if we know he was lying," Sommers continued, "that means he had something to lie about. That business is the only thing we have connecting Tommy to anything illegal."

"Other than recreational drug use," Raine pointed out.

"He wasn't murdered because of recreational drug use," Sommers said, dismissing the idea. "He was murdered because he knew something. Something someone didn't want out. Something illegal. And that place is definitely doing something illegal."

"Tommy probably saw something when he was making a delivery there," Raine surmised. "That would explain the address, the cash, and his death. He delivered whatever it was, got paid, then got the hell out of there but not before seeing something he shouldn't have."

"If we can figure out what that something was," Sommers continued, "you can give that to your prosecutor and get your case dismissed."

Raine frowned. "I'm not sure how it connects to his death sufficiently to convince her to dismiss it."

"Of course you don't," Sommers answered. "We haven't gone there yet."

Raine had to laugh at the undeniable logic.

"You said your prosecutor wants to dismiss the case, right?" Sommers pressed him.

"She said she doesn't care if she dismisses it," Raine clarified, "so long as it doesn't get dismissed on my motion for vindictive prosecution."

"So give her something, anything," Sommers said, "and let her figure out how it leads to a dismissal."

Raine sighed. He knew she was right. He knew what he had to do. And he knew what he had to say.

"Sorry, Rebecca. I'm just not convinced," he lied. "I'll have to think of something else."

18

R aine waited for the weekend. He supposed there was a chance Axis Global Import-Export might be closed on the weekend, or at least have shorter hours. He also waited for nightfall. In part, for cover of darkness. In part, because when he'd gone to scope the place out on Saturday afternoon, they were very definitely open. So he'd made himself scarce and returned after nightfall. By then, it was raining. A good solid rain, not just a mist most Seattleites wouldn't even notice. Raine was glad for it. Darkness meant no light. A hard rain meant no people.

Raine sat in his car, parked up the street from Pier 32, but just close enough that he could still see the front of the warehouse. He just needed to wait for Armand Kasaybian to close up for the night, then wait another hour to make sure he didn't come back for something he'd forgotten.

Kasaybian emerged from his building at approximately 6:50 p.m. He wasn't alone. He and the other person spent several minutes in dialogue in the downpour.

Raine supposed it must have been important if they were

willing to get drenched to renew a conversation they could have had inside. From that distance, Raine couldn't make out anything about the other person other than that they were shorter than Kasaybian, but then so were most people.

Eventually they finished their conversation and went their separate ways. The other person to an older American sedan parked down the road, and Kasaybian to his late-model European sports car parked at the pier. Both of them drove away, Kasaybian's car passing as Raine ducked below the window line of his own car.

Raine waited a little more than an hour to make sure neither Kasaybian nor his contact returned. By 8:00 p.m., the tourist waterfront to the north was still filled with people and activity, but the working waterfront of Pier 32 was empty. He waited another thirty minutes until it felt desolate. Then he stepped out of the car and into the rain. He had some crime to commit.

In truth, he was going to do his best not to commit any crimes. Not any felonies anyway. He was not about to break into the warehouse. But if Kasaybian had left the door unlocked again, he would have a defense under the law that he reasonably believed he was permitted to be there. What else could you conclude from an unlocked door? Or hopefully two unlocked doors. He was curious what was on the other side of the door Kasaybian had emerged from at their last meeting. If the doors were unlocked, at most it would be trespassing, and he could talk his way out of a trespassing charge. Probably.

Raine pulled his hood over his head and hunched forward against the rain. He'd dressed for the weather, with a heavy coat and waterproof shoes. There was no one else on the street as he walked back toward Pier 32. The only other car parked on the road was an older American sedan several hundred feet north. Raine suspected it might be abandoned; it didn't even have plates on it. His footsteps slapped in the puddles that collected in the uneven pavement.

He was relieved to reach the edge of the wooden pier. The wood was a bit slippery, but it was quiet. There was a row of waist-high metal posts designed to keep vehicle traffic off the pier. They were connected by a loosely hanging metal chain. Raine took note that the chain didn't completely cordon off the pier, and he deliberately walked to the end of the posts, and their connecting chain, to enter the pier, rather than step over the chain.

The pier felt even more desolate than the empty street. There were only two lampposts illuminating the dock, and their light didn't reach far enough to prevent large swaths of darkness. Raine had been waiting long enough that his eyes had adjusted to the darkness, and there was light pollution from downtown, so he could navigate the darkened areas. Even so, he somehow felt both very alone and very vulnerable to being seen. He hurried to the one and only door in the front of the warehouse.

He stared at the doorknob for a moment. If it was unlocked, he'd have a credible claim that he thought it was permissible to go inside. It would also suggest that Kasaybian didn't have anything to hide, and he was probably on a wild-goose chase anyway. He wasn't sure which result he wanted. So he reached out and turned the knob, leaving the result to fate. Or Kasaybian, really.

It was locked. Of course.

Even if Kasaybian wasn't doing anything illegal out of the building, it was still a business, with machinery and electronics and other assets. The locked door only proved Kasaybian wasn't stupid or reckless. But Raine had known that as soon as he met the man.

He stepped back and wiped away the rain that had dripped onto his face from his hood. *Now what?*

There weren't any windows on the front of the building, and the back of it went all the way to the edge of the dock. He turned the corner and confirmed the wall farthest from the road also had no doors or windows. That left the long wall extending up from the edge of the pier. He leaned against the slippery wood of the wall and leaned out over the water to scan the back of the building. To both his delight and dismay, there was a series of windows running the length of the building. They would allow him to see what was really housed inside the mysterious business. If he didn't fall into the Sound.

There was a single raised plank, the width of a shoe, that acted as a sort of curb between the building wall and the icy water below. It would be just enough for Raine to inch his way to the windows. The building blocked what little light there was from the lampposts, so Raine would have to rely on the ambient light pollution to see anything. That wasn't particularly impactful, however, because he couldn't see anything other than the wall anyway as he flattened himself against the wet building and began carefully shuffling down the worn, slippery beam.

The rain stabbed at the backs of Raine's outstretched hands. The water from the side of the building rubbed against his face and down his neck. He imagined the hot shower he would take when he got home and assured himself the adventure would be worth it. What had Tommy delivered? And would it be obvious when Raine saw it? He was about to find out. After several feet of sliding himself along the frigid wood, Raine reached the first window. He really hoped it didn't have curtains.

There were no curtains. But the lights weren't on either. Raine grasped the edges of the window frame and stared into the darkened warehouse, waiting for his eyes to adjust enough to see something. Anything. After a few moments, he thought he could make out the shape of stacked boxes and crowded shelving. Nothing obviously illegal. Nothing really recognizable, actually. Literal black boxes in the dark of the night, their contents inscrutable.

"Maybe the next room," Raine told himself.

The rainwater from the side of the building had soaked its way through his jacket to his skin. He fought off the urge to shiver, lest the movement throw him off balance and he slip off his toehold.

He pushed himself past the first window and slowly made his way toward the second window. There were three windows in all, he could see. One way or another, he'd be done soon and on his way to his warm apartment.

The second window also didn't have curtains. It did have blinds though, and those were very much closed. The window offered Raine nothing more than a change in the type of wood he was pressing his increasingly wet and cold face against. The tip of his nose was going numb. He shook against the rain pummeling his back and pressed on toward the final window. The warehouse hadn't seemed so unceasingly long when he had been standing safely on the other side of it.

The final window had curtains, but they weren't drawn completely closed. There was a several-inch gap in the middle, although part of that was taken up by the wooden crosspiece of the window frame. Nevertheless, Raine was able to peer inside, aided by the fact that someone had left on a small desk lamp on the far side of the room. There was enough light to make out several tables with packaging equipment: scales, baggies, small bottles, tape. There wasn't anything on the tables that would have ended up in those baggies and bottles; that part had been cleaned up. But Raine could guess. Tommy hadn't been making deliveries to Axis Global Import-Export. He had been picking them up.

Excited to be finished with his quest, Raine pushed off the window a little too hard, and one of his feet slid completely off the wooden rail. He grasped at the window frame with his fingertips and barely managed not to fall backward into the churning icy black water below.

He took a moment for his heart to slow. Then he slowly and carefully made his way to the end of the building and stepped back onto the relative safety of the full dock.

Then Kasaybian shoved him into the water.

Raine hit the water back first and immediately felt his body begin to freeze up in the icy current. He struggled to right himself and get his head above water as his drenched clothes tried to pull him under. He splashed and paddled his way back to the dock where there was a ladder bolted to one of the posts. He grabbed ahold of the metal and looked up at the dock. He couldn't see Kasaybian, but he knew he was there. But there was no other way out of the water. The Sound ended in a retaining wall, not a beach. The way out was up. And the way home was through Kasaybian. Raine was okay with that. Kasaybian was taller, but Raine was bigger. And he was pissed.

But Kasaybian was smart. He wasn't alone.

When Raine pulled his drenched body to the top of the ladder, water running like a river from his clothing back into the Puget Sound, he was greeted by the sight of Kasaybian standing behind three masked men. Three large, masked men.

He knew what was about to happen. But he was going to get his licks in too.

If Kasaybian wanted him dead, he would have been dead already. Or at least kicked off the top of the ladder and into the water again. No, Kasaybian wanted to teach him a lesson. A silent lesson, it seemed. He didn't say anything, to Raine or to his goons. He just nodded once, and they advanced.

As the men approached slowly, Raine took the opportunity to move away from the edge of the dock and get his back against the wall of the warehouse. But he wasn't going to have enough time to pull off his waterlogged jacket. His heavy clothes were going to make his movements slow and plodding. He wasn't going to be able to exchange blows. He needed to grapple, and maybe he could hurt one of them enough to distract the others. If they even cared about each other enough to be distracted by that. But it was his only chance.

Raine lowered himself into a ready crouch, bracing a foot against the wall behind him. "All right. Come on, you cowards," he taunted. "Who's gonna be first?"

Of course they didn't line up to take him on one at a time. That only happened in the movies. In the docks, they rushed him all at once. So Raine grabbed the one who got there first around the waist and pulled him to the ground with him. He managed to spin on top of the man and began punching him in the face as hard as he could. He felt flesh and bone give way under his fist, but he only got three or four blows in before the other two grabbed his arms and pulled him off their compatriot. Still, that compatriot didn't get up, and suddenly it was only two against one. The odds were improving.

One of the men reached under Raine's arms from behind and pinned him so the other man could pummel him. Raine took a punch to the mouth, then a series to his stomach and sides. He knew the blows to his torso were coming, so he managed to avoid having the wind knocked out of him, but he wasn't going to be able to withstand much more.

He jerked his head back fast and hard, hoping to smash the nose of the man behind him. The man managed to dodge Raine's skull, but in so doing, his grip loosened, and Raine was able to slip out of his grasp. He turned and delivered a punch to the side of the man's head, sending the already off-balance man stumbling.

The other man then jumped on Raine's back. Raine allowed himself to be driven to the wooden deck and attempted again to get on top of his opponent. He couldn't quite manage it, however, as the man sat on his back and punched the back of his head repeatedly, smashing Raine's face into the rain-soaked planks.

Raine tried to push himself onto his hands and knees, but the man he'd sent stumbling had returned, and Raine was forced to use his hands to cover his face and head as the man started to kick him. He suspected he was going to get his ribs cracked, or worse, as the man's boot drove repeatedly into his side.

Raine still had enough senses to notice that the third man, the one whose nose Raine had likely broken to start the fight, had also regained himself. Three sets of fists and boots hailed down on him, joining the freezing cold rain that hadn't let up the entire night. Raine wondered whether Kasaybian maybe did want him dead after all.

Then three things happened that were so completely unexpected that Raine thought he might be hallucinating from the pain.

First, the strobe and wail of a police car lit up the dock. Second, his assailants disappeared into the night. Third, Kasaybian stepped out of the shadows and onto Raine's back. He shoved the tip of a cane into Raine's jaw.

"Over here, Officers!" Kasaybian called out. "This is the man I called about. Hurry, before he tries to get away!"

Raine couldn't even feel his frozen and bruised legs. He wasn't going anywhere. Not on his own, anyway.

Two burly police officers rushed over to his location and slapped handcuffs on him without any regard whatsoever for his injuries.

He let out a yelp of pain, but the officers showed no concern.

"Be quiet, you," one of them warned as they pulled Raine to his feet. "You're under arrest."

"For what?" Raine asked through a fat lip.

"Burglary for one thing," the other officer answered. "I'm sure we'll think of more on the way to the jail."

19

"**B**urglary. Assault. Menacing." The sergeant on the other side of the table in the interrogation room ticked off a series of offenses on his fingertips. He was in his mid-thirties, with swollen biceps under his stripes and a thick mustache over his grin. "You're in a lot of trouble, pal."

Raine was able to deduce several facts from the sergeant's opening gambit. Raine knew there was no crime called "menacing," at least not in Washington State. That meant the sergeant didn't really have anything on him. It also meant the sergeant didn't know Raine was a lawyer. And all of that meant he wasn't really in that much trouble after all, pal.

"Can we cut to the part where you let me go?" Raine asked. "I'll even forego the apology. I just have a lot to do, and I don't want to waste an entire night sitting in a jail cell."

"You're looking at wasting a lot more than one night, my friend." The sergeant shook his head at Raine. "You'd better start talking and tell me what really happened out there, or you're looking at spending a few hundred nights in jail. Do you know what the sentence for felony assault is?"

He did, in fact.

Raine sighed. He needed information. And probably some stitches. In that order, apparently. But he was unlikely to get either talking to just a sergeant.

"Call Detective Gillespie," Raine instructed. "Tell him I have information about the fatal accident down on Alaskan Way."

"Gillespie?" the sergeant questioned.

"Yes," Raine confirmed. "Leo Gillespie. He's a homicide detective."

The sergeant laughed. "Gillespie's not a homicide detective. He's in narcotics."

"Narcotics?" Raine didn't understand. "Why was he investigating a death scene?"

"Good question," the sergeant said. "What were you doing at a death scene?"

An even better question, Raine supposed.

"Are you a drug addict or something?" the sergeant asked. "Is that why you were out on an empty pier after dark?"

Or something, Raine thought. "I'm not a drug addict. And I didn't do anything illegal tonight, even if it was after dark."

"I'd say burglary is illegal," the sergeant scoffed.

"Burglary requires an entry into a building," Raine replied. "I never went inside."

"The law defines a building as including any fenced-in area," the sergeant argued.

"Yes. Revised Code of Washington, Title 9A, Chapter 4, Section 110." Raine cited the relevant statute. "But the chain fencing off the entrance to the pier didn't extend all the way to the end."

The sergeant frowned and lifted his chin slightly. "Well, it was still trespassing."

"It is a defense to the charge of trespassing that the premises were open to the public or the actor reasonably believed the owner would have licensed him to enter or remain on the premises." Raine reeled off the language of the relevant statute before citing it. "Revised Code of Washington 9A.52.090."

The sergeant narrowed his eyes at Raine. "You a lawyer or something?"

"Or something," Raine answered. He'd learned what he was likely to from this cop. It was time to move on. "So why don't we cut to the part where you let me go because you don't have any evidence? And if you don't have the guts to do that, then I'll post the booking bail for whatever crime you were thinking of booking me on. Do you need the citation for the statewide statutory bail schedule? I'll give you a hint. It's in Title 9."

Suddenly, the sergeant became very obviously uncomfortable. He had expected to be in charge of the interview. Obviously, he was not. His indecision was palpable.

"Take your time," Raine prompted. "I'm going to need someone to attend to these wounds though. I think we'd both prefer I took care of that somewhere other than your jail. I'm a lawyer, remember. I know how to sue you and everyone involved for false arrest, malicious prosecution. Throw in a medical malpractice claim and I'll be able to retire. Do you own a home, Sergeant"—Raine leaned forward to read the officer's name tag—"Sherman? You might not after I get done with you."

Sergeant Sherman stood up abruptly. "Stay here," he instructed, as if Raine could go anywhere from inside the jail while handcuffed.

Raine nodded his assent, and the sergeant went out to consult with his superiors. It took several minutes, which Raine used to consider his next steps—after urgent care— but eventually Sergeant Sherman returned. With a set of handcuff keys.

"It's your lucky day, Mr. Raine," the sergeant said, using his name for the first time. He must have asked around. Apparently J. Daniel Raine, attorney at law, had a reputation with the Seattle Police Department.

"You're letting me go because I'm so obviously innocent?"

"No," the sergeant seemed happy to say as he unlocked Raine's handcuffs. "You made bail."

Raine rubbed his unshackled wrists. "Made bail? But you haven't even given me the chance."

"Someone posted the booking bail for burglary," Sherman explained. "If the prosecutor decides to file charges, you'll get a summons in the mail."

Raine knew that. He also thought he knew who posted his bail. "Is Ms. Mount in the lobby?" She had no reason to know where he was, but he supposed if anyone might be missing him and was smart enough to figure out where he was, it was Sawyer.

"Mount?" Sherman frowned at him. "I'm not sure who that is. The lady who posted your bail is named Sommers."

Raine smiled. *Or Sommers.*

"HOLY CRAP!" Sommers exclaimed as Raine emerged into the precinct lobby. His face was covered in cuts and bruises, and the jail hadn't offered him any fresh clothes. His shirt and pants weren't dripping anymore, but they weren't dry either.

"I could say the same to you," Raine replied over the cut in his lip. "How did you know I was here?"

Sommers grinned sideways at him. "Private investigator trade secret."

Raine was in no mood. "Not good enough. You're not even a real private investigator."

Sommers crossed her arms. "I disagree. I faked it long enough that I think I made it."

Raine didn't want to argue that particular point. "Seriously, though. It might be important for me to know. Did I make the news or something?"

"Oh, Dan, no." Sommers laughed. "You're not that important. No, after our little talk the other day, I thought you might do something stupid without me, so I made the most basic investment in a police scanner radio. I would just leave it on while I did paperwork. Do you have any idea how many police callouts there are every hour? And how many of them are petrifyingly boring?"

Raine had a very good idea about both of those things.

"But then I heard officers being dispatched to a burglary and assault in progress at Axis Global Import-Export," Sommers continued. "That was just so obviously you."

Raine nodded. He didn't like being obvious—no one did, he expected—but she wasn't wrong.

"So I listened to all of the radio traffic," she went on, "until you were brought to the downtown precinct and the call was closed out."

"Did I sound tough?" Raine wondered. "Like, the cops

sent a bunch of officers to handle the big guy beating people up on the pier?"

Sommers's lips twisted into a tight frown. "Um, no. No, it sounded like you got your ass handed to you, and the cops just needed to scrape you off the dock."

"Yeah, that's probably accurate," Raine admitted. "But I did get a few good licks in. Pretty sure I broke at least one nose." Then he touched his own tender nose. "Then again, they may have too."

"Good for you." Sommers patted him on the shoulder. Then she held her damp hand out awkwardly to the side, evidently unsure how to dry it without wiping it on her expensive and delicate ensemble. After a moment, she shook it once and lowered it to her side, but a few inches away from her body. "Well, then I called Sawyer and—"

"You called Sawyer?" Raine cried. "Why did you do that?"

"I'm a private investigator, remember? Not a lawyer. I had no idea what to do next, but she explained how to get you out right away before they booked you into the jail and you went in front of a judge tomorrow to have your bail jacked up tenfold."

That was the usual procedure. Raine sighed. His embarrassment at being beaten up and arrested was outweighed by his relief at being released. "Did you tell her I got my ass handed to me?"

Sommers pulled an imaginary zipper across her lips. "Trade secret. You can tell her whatever you want about the fight." She looked him up and down again. "Maybe after you clean up a bit."

"Is she coming down here?" Raine asked. He did want a chance to clean himself up before seeing his girlfriend.

"No, she said I could handle it." Sommers eased his concern. "She knows I'm a real investigator."

"She knows it's eleven o'clock at night and didn't want to spend her night with a bunch of cops." Raine rubbed his sore wrists again. "Not that I blame her. I'm ready to get out of here too. Can I bother you for a ride home?"

He considered asking for that ride to urgent care, but he just wanted to get home and get some sleep. He would still be injured in the morning.

"Of course, Dan." Sommers scoffed. "What are partners for?"

Raine considered arguing about the correct label for their relationship, but in that moment Sommers felt very much like a partner.

They exited the precinct and started the walk up Fifth Avenue. The rain had diminished to a light drizzle.

"Did you at least find what you were looking for?" Sommers asked. "What was inside the warehouse?"

Raine shook his head. "I never went inside."

Sommers halted her gait. "You never went inside? How did you get arrested for burglary, then? And more importantly, why the hell not?"

"So I wouldn't get arrested for burglary," Raine answered. "Or at least not get convicted of it. There were windows around back. I snuck along the edge of the dock and peered in the windows."

"That's weak," Sommers judged as she started them walking again.

"That's smart," Raine argued. "The cops really don't have anything on me. Kasaybian, on the other hand. He definitely has the upper hand on us now."

"Was he there?"

"He's the one who pushed me into the Sound," Raine answered. "And he's the one who had three goons waiting to beat me up when I climbed out. I thought I was careful, but he must have seen me. And now he knows I know something."

"What do you know?"

"Well, more like suspect," Raine corrected. "I mean, I only got a glimpse into a dark room through a rainy window."

"Fine, what do you suspect?" Sommers amended her question.

Raine nodded. "It's a front for a drug operation."

They had reached her car parked in a three-minute loading zone, of course. And not ticketed, of course. Some people had all the luck.

"Didn't we kind of already suspect that?" she asked as she opened the driver's door.

"We did," Raine agreed as he climbed into the front passenger seat. "But now we suspect it even more."

"And Kasaybian suspects you now," Sommers pointed out.

"That does seem to be the main development from my adventure on Pier 32," Raine acknowledged. "But then I learned something else when I interrogated the cop."

"You mean when the cop interrogated you?" Sommers questioned.

"No, he didn't get anything from me," Raine said, "except maybe a quick lesson on the finer points of burglary law. But he told me something we didn't know that may mean a deeper connection between Kasaybian and Tommy than just a simple drug delivery."

"Do tell," Sommers encouraged as she pulled into the roadway.

"Remember that detective who showed up at the scene after Porter got smeared down half a block of Alaskan Way?"

Sommers grimaced. "Lovely way to put it. Yeah, what about him? He seemed interested in the case. Was it not a typical fatal accident?"

"It was probably pretty typical," Raine allowed, "but Detective Gillespie isn't a homicide detective."

"Accident reconstruction?" Sommers guessed.

"Drugs," Raine told her. "And do you know what narcotics detectives do with drug runners?"

"Arrest them?" Sommers ventured.

"Flip them," Raine told her. "Turn them into informants."

"You think Gillespie was using Tommy as an informant?" Sommers asked.

"That might explain why he showed up at the death of a witness to Tommy's death," Raine suggested.

"But that would mean that he knew Porter was working that night," Sommers realized. "Would a detective just naturally know that sort of thing?"

"With a hundred arrestees processed every day and a thousand more housed there?" Raine responded. "No way. Not unless he had a special interest in Tommy being in jail."

Sommers looked over at Raine, her platinum hair haloed by the passing streetlights. "And a special interest in him never getting out again."

Raine nodded, his thoughts falling into line.

"So what next?" Sommers asked. "Confront Gillespie? Go to the prosecutor?"

"The prosecutor?" Raine laughed. "They'll never help me

take down a cop. They work for the cops. And no, it's too early to confront Gillespie. It's bad enough Kasaybian knows I'm onto him. I don't need to tip off Gillespie too."

"So what's next?" Sommers repeated.

"Next." Raine nodded to himself. "Next I have a motion to win."

20

R aine and Ophelia arrived promptly at Judge Taylor's courtroom for the hearing on their motion to dismiss the criminal case for vindictive prosecution. "Promptly" meant fifteen minutes early. 8:45 a.m. The courtroom was open, but no one else was there yet. Even the bailiff and court reporter were back in chambers.

Raine set up his things on the defendant's table. Ophelia just sat down, looking unsure of what else to do.

He gave her a legal pad and a pen. "Take notes," he instructed.

"Will that help you?" she asked hopefully.

"No," Raine admitted. "But it will keep you busy, and that will help you."

Ophelia smiled, then slid the pad in front of her. She hovered the pen over the top line, but then set it down again without writing anything.

Before Raine could offer any suggestions for headings, the door from the hallway opened, and in walked Deputy District Attorney Catherine Tennet. Behind her walked in a troop of other prosecutors, ten at least. They were identifiable as prosecutors by their bland suits and humorless expressions. The oldest of them, a man with a particularly mirthless countenance, sat directly behind the prosecution table in the first row of the gallery.

Tennet walked up to the prosecution table, set her briefcase down on it, then stepped over to Raine. "You never called me," she whispered. "I thought you were going to give me a reason to dismiss this before we had to do the hearing."

Raine turned and sized up the crowd Tennet had brought with her. "That your boss?" he whispered back. "He looks stressed."

"Yes, that's my boss," Tennet confirmed. "Phil Salazar, chief of our violent crimes unit. He's, like, two steps from being the big boss."

"Violent crimes?" Raine questioned. "She's a middle-aged woman who got jumped by the cops."

"Assault is a violent crime," Tennet argued back. "But that's not why he's here. He's here as management. If I lose this, the big boss wants to know immediately."

"To congratulate me?" Raine quipped.

"To fire me," Tennet answered. "Then immediately into damage control. This case is already bad press for us. A judicial determination of bad faith by the cops—"

"And you," Raine interjected.

Tennet sighed. "A judicial determination of bad faith by the cops, and the prosecutors, is exactly what we don't need right now."

"When would you need it?" Raine kept up the humor. It was almost 9:00, and Tennet hadn't even unpacked her briefcase. She was nowhere near the right frame of mind to argue the motion. Advantage: Raine.

"What I needed was a reason to dismiss this case and avoid exactly what is happening now," Tennet hissed. She nodded at the still healing bruises on Raine's cheek and nose. "I heard you got arrested. Did my cops do that to you?"

Raine laughed. "As much as I'd like to add myself as a plaintiff to Ms. Wilson's lawsuit against the police department, no. But you should see the other guys."

"Were you trying to get me something?" Tennet was grasping. "We could agree to set over this hearing. Tell the judge that new evidence has been discovered."

"I don't have any new evidence for you," Raine told her.

"Is in the process of being discovered," Tennet amended. She glanced at Phil Salazar.

Raine did too. His frown was absolutely carved into his face.

"I've got nothing," Raine repeated. "Let's just do this. What are the odds that an elected judge will actually dismiss a case against someone accused of assaulting the police? Doesn't your office give him a bunch of money for his re-election campaign every four years?"

"Everybody gives him a bunch of money," Tennet answered. "The defense bar has a hell of a lot more rich lawyers than an office full of government lawyers."

"Then may the best not-rich lawyer win." Raine extended his hand to her.

She looked at it, then again at Salazar, then apparently decided not to be even professional lest it be interpreted as friendliness to the enemy. She didn't shake. Instead, she huffed and turned back to her counsel table.

The bailiff entered the court and called the courtroom to order. "All rise! The King County Superior Court is now in session, the Honorable Lucas Taylor presiding!"

Judge Taylor marched to the bench and sat down briskly. "Please be seated," he instructed. He surveyed the courtroom and frowned at the small crowd assembled. "I see we have an audience for today's hearing. I will assume it arises from an interest in the subject matter and not a desire to intimidate the judge."

Raine was already liking the hearing.

"Are the parties ready on the matter of *The State of Washington versus Ophelia Wilson*?" the judge asked. It was mostly perfunctory, but things did come up sometimes. Tennet had been counting on it.

She stood and practically admitted, "The State is ready, Your Honor."

Raine followed suit, standing to confirm, "The defense is ready."

"Excellent." Taylor rubbed his hands together. "Our audience will not be disappointed. Well, not until my ruling perhaps."

Raine's hopes increased further.

"This is the defendant's motion," Judge Taylor stated, "so I will hear first from the defense. Whenever you're ready, Mr. Raine."

Raine was definitely ready. He wanted nothing more than a dismissal in the criminal case, if only so he didn't have to try two cases back-to-back. That was an all-day, all-week, all-month endeavor. It was nearly impossible to accept new clients because he wouldn't be able to attend their court dates. He preferred not to turn business away for weeks on end, even with the possibility of a big payday at the end of the civil trial. There was no guarantee he would win that. Juries could be unpredictable. Lawyers always preferred asking a judge for what they wanted.

"Thank you, Your Honor," Raine answered.

He had remained standing after his confirmation of readiness. Tennet sat down and stared at him. Ophelia picked up her pen, but still didn't write anything.

"The defendant, Ms. Wilson, is asking this honorable Court to dismiss the criminal charges brought against her by the King County Prosecutor's Office on behalf of the State of Washington," Raine began. "We are asking for this extraordinary remedy because it is the correct, just and indeed only remedy permitted when the criminal charges were brought as part of a vindictive prosecution. And this prosecution against Ms. Wilson is the textbook definition of a vindictive prosecution."

That wasn't exactly true, Raine knew. Taylor knew it too. And Tennet. And all three of them knew the others knew it. But this was argument. Hyperbole was to be expected, if not outright encouraged, if only to inject a human element into what could be the dusty, deadened discipline of the Law.

"Now, to be sure," Raine quickly qualified his assertion, "there are a limited number of published cases that address this particular doctrine."

"I counted three," Judge Taylor interrupted.

Raine had found two. That was why Taylor was the judge. "Precisely, Your Honor. And while it might seem that such a dearth of case law might make it difficult to discern the proper ruling in this case, allow me to suggest that those three cases are so tightly aligned that the Court can easily craft the rule for when a case should be dismissed, and then see how clearly this case fits that rule."

Taylor frowned slightly, but he didn't say anything. Instead, he simply leaned back in his chair, which was an invitation for Raine to continue.

"The test, as outlined in those cases, is whether the charges were filed in response to, in retaliation for, and as punishment for the defendant's exercise of a Constitutionally protected right. So it's not sufficient that the defendant may have done just anything to annoy the police or the prosecutor. If charges were filed in response to a defendant, say, refusing to donate to the annual policeman's ball, that would be terrible, unconscionable even, but it would not fall under the rule for vindictive prosecution.

"On the other hand, it is also irrelevant if the charges have factual support, that is, that there is evidence the defendant actually committed the crime. The reason that is irrelevant is that any case that doesn't have at least some evidence to support the charge should, in theory anyway, be dismissed by other means. And I would submit, this is part of the reason why there are so few cases of this type that make it to the appellate courts. It needs to be a case that does have factual support, but was brought not to enforce the laws generally, but to punish the defendant specifically, and to punish them not for the crime committed, but for daring to exercise some legal right enshrined in the state or federal constitution. That will almost never happen. It should never happen. But it did happen in this case, Your Honor."

Raine took a moment to read the room. Judge Taylor was listening intently. He was leaning back in his chair, but his hand was to his face, with a thoughtful index finger extended along the side of his nose. Phil Salazar still wasn't smiling, and his cadre of denizens followed his lead. Ophelia still hadn't written anything on her legal pad. And Tennet was still just staring at him.

Raine preferred not to eyeball his opponent in open court, at least not in front of the jury. It could come across as overly aggressive or even just strange. Raine wondered whether Tennet would do it again when he was giving his opening statement to the jury—assuming he lost the dismissal motion, of course.

"In this case," Raine continued, "Ms. Wilson has been charged with a plethora of thinly supported, imaginatively crafted criminal charges, all in retaliation for her exercise of her constitutionally protected rights to freedom of speech, freedom to peaceably assemble, and freedom to petition the government for redress of grievances."

He paused. The Law could indeed be dusty and deadened. It was good to remind everyone that it involved actual people. "Her son is dead, Your Honor." Raine let his voice crack ever so slightly.

Taylor sat forward again.

"He died in police custody," Raine went on. "And no one would tell her how or why. They still haven't told her how or why. I deposed the medical examiner who conducted the autopsy, and he won't even tell us. And so, Your Honor, we have a mother who lost her child and who was told there would be no comment, no explanation, no justice.

"What else was she supposed to do? Just go home and accept that the jail had killed her son and she'd never know what happened? She would never know what his last moments were like. Not because no one knew, but because no one would tell her. No, Your Honor, Ms. Wilson couldn't accept that.

"And she didn't have to accept that. Our constitution gives us the right to protest against the government. It is probably the most important right we have because it is the one that allows us to change the government. The one that allows us to shed light on injustice, enlist others to our cause, and try to make our nation better. It was for the exercise of this right that she now faces charges that have the potential of sending her to state prison for years. All because she wouldn't shut up and take it."

Raine looked down at his client. She was finally writing something: "Amen."

"First the police told her to be quiet. Then they told her to leave. Then they arrested her. Then they charged her. We're all familiar with the term 'overcharging.' That's when a prosecutor charges the absolutely most serious crime the facts could possibly fit. Charging a shoplifter with robbery because he pushed the clerk on the way out the door, or charging a trespasser with burglary because there was a fence somewhere encircling the property."

Raine took a moment to see if Tennet reacted, but she kept her unblinking gaze on him. She must not have read his police report yet.

"And so this case presents another case of overcharging," he continued. "Although I am actually grateful for the draconian decision to charge Ms. Wilson with so many and so serious of crimes. Had she been charged with a single count of, say, disorderly conduct, the vindictiveness would be less apparent. But here, we have the imaginative decision to charge Ms. Wilson with the felony of Intimidation of a Public Servant for daring to ask the police not to arrest her. We have the truly unjustifiable decision to charge felony assault on an officer for trying to recover the photo of her dead son that the officer snatched from her mourning hands. I thank the State for reaching so far that it exposed their true intention. To quiet Ms. Wilson and to scare her into accepting a plea bargain so she didn't bring the exact motion before Your Honor today."

Raine took a deep breath. He was almost done. Everyone was listening to him. He really did enjoy that part of being a trial attorney. He hoped he would get the other thing he really liked: a favorable ruling.

"So, in conclusion, Your Honor," Raine wrapped up, "we ask the Court to apply the facts of this case to the rule against vindictive prosecution. We believe the Court will agree that this case was filed in violation of that rule. And we pray the Court will grant our motion to dismiss. Thank you."

There was no applause—the gallery was hostile to his position—but Raine got a pat on the arm and a "Thank you" from his client as he sat down. Better than applause, he decided.

Judge Taylor swung his head toward the prosecution table. "Ms. Tennet, your response?"

Tennet had finally stopped staring at Raine. He guessed it might have been to avoid repeated nervous glances at Salazar. She stood and tugged her suitcoat into place. "The State asks the Court to deny the defendant's motion to dismiss," she began.

It was always good to start with what you wanted the judge to do. The "ask."

"The motion is not well grounded in facts or law," Tennet said. "Dismissal for vindictive prosecution is an extraordinary remedy for an extraordinary claim. It should be reserved for the most egregious instances of governmental misconduct. This is not that case."

Just regular government misconduct, Raine thought. He wasn't staring at Tennet. He was keeping his head down and taking notes. Ophelia's pad still only had that one word on it.

"The most significant flaw to the defendant's argument," Tennet continued, "is the timeline. Vindictive prosecution is a doctrine to hold prosecutors accountable, but the initial decisions in this case were all made by law enforcement, specifically the corrections officers of the King County Jail. They are an entirely separate agency and have no impact on our charging decisions whatsoever."

Taylor raised an eyebrow. "Don't law enforcement officers decide what charges to book a suspect in and what charges to refer to your office for charging?"

"They do, Your Honor," Tennet conceded, "but we are not involved in the decision to book, and we are not bound by the recommended charges. We can, and do, decline to file charges in many cases. In others, we charge something other than what is recommended by law enforcement."

Taylor's raised eyebrow was joined by an incredulous frown. "Aren't those the exceptions that prove the rule? The vast majority of cases you file are the charges recommended to you by law enforcement, isn't that true? And isn't that what happened in this case?"

Raine suppressed the urge to shout out, *Yeah!* He wrote it on his notepad instead.

"It is what usually happens," Tennet conceded, "but it is not precisely what happened in this case. We did file all of the recommended charges, but we also added charges of intimidation of a public servant and disorderly conduct."

"Your office added those to what was recommended by the cops?"

"Yes, Your Honor," Tennet answered.

Taylor pursed his lips and nodded several times. "I don't think that helps your argument, counsel. But please continue."

"Uh..." Tennet hesitated.

Raine knew she needed a moment to regain her argument. Nothing throws an advocate off quite like a judge criticizing it before it was even finished. Especially when the advocate's boss was in the front row.

"So, as I was saying," Tennet continued, "the timing in this case does not support the defendant's argument. The defendant committed several crimes, was arrested for those crimes, then was charged with those crimes. Very standard and in no way vindictive."

"Would you agree with the proposition," Judge Taylor interrupted again, "that all prosecutions are at least partially vindictive in nature?"

Raine frowned. It sounded like another jab at Tennet's argument, but it was actually a lifeline. Raine wondered whether Tennet would realize that.

"I... would, Your Honor," she realized to say. "Prosecution for a crime inherently involves imposing a punishment for prior behavior. So, to prevail, Mr. Raine needs to show more than just that the prosecution might have a vindictive, or retributive, aspect. He has failed to do so. And he has failed to offer this Court any rationale for why the police or prosecutors would bother doing so. Ms. Wilson's case is undoubtedly important to her. And I can sympathize with the loss of her child. But hers is one of literally thousands of felony cases we file every year in King County. There are tens of thousands more misdemeanors. Honestly, Your Honor, I have more than enough to do without looking to be vindictive against a woman who lost her son to some unsolved tragedy."

Finally, a human element to her argument, Raine thought. *Damn.*

"That's not how I do things, Your Honor." Tennet glanced at her colleagues in the gallery. "That's not how my office does things. And that's not what happened here. Accordingly, the Court should deny the defendant's motion to dismiss and allow the case to proceed to trial next week. Thank you."

Taylor nodded several times again and leaned forward. "This is a very interesting issue," he began. "A rare one, which is part of what makes it interesting." A gesture to the gallery. "And it's interesting to more than just the two lawyers who argued it. I understand the gravity of my ruling. The defendant isn't simply asking to have her case dismissed on some legal technicality. If I grant this motion, I will not be simply dismissing a single criminal case. I will be rendering a judicial determination that the prosecutor's office engaged in the worst sort of perversion of justice."

Raine nodded. That was exactly what he was asking for.

"Mr. Raine." The judge pointed down at him. "You mentioned conducting a deposition regarding events related to this case. Is there a civil case as well?"

"There is, Your Honor." Raine stood up. "I represent Ms. Wilson in that matter as well. It's a civil suit for the wrongful death of her son."

"When is that set for trial?" Taylor asked.

"Immediately after the criminal case, Your Honor," Raine answered. "The criminal case has to go first. Ms. Wilson has the right to remain silent in the criminal case, but not the civil. The criminal case needs to be finished, one way or another, before we can start a trial when Ms. Wilson will testify about the impact of losing her son."

Taylor nodded again, judicial gears spinning behind his eyes. "Time is of the essence, then."

"I suppose so, Your Honor," Raine agreed. "We await the Court's ruling."

Judge Taylor smiled at that. "Well, I'm afraid you're all going to have to wait a little bit longer. Sorry, Mr. Salazar." A nod to the gallery. "But I am not about to rule on a motion of this magnitude without taking sufficient time to fully consider the arguments presented here today."

That was not ideal. "Trial is in one week, Your Honor. It would be good to know whether we really need to prepare for it."

"Oh, definitely prepare for it, Mr. Raine," the judge answered. "You too, Ms. Tennet. I can honestly say that I haven't decided how I am going to rule. But I can say with absolute certainty that I expect both parties to be in my courtroom at nine a.m. sharp one week from today, at which time I will deliver my ruling."

Then to make sure everyone understood, he rapped his gavel on the bench. "Court is adjourned."

Raine cursed under his breath.

"What just happened?" Ophelia asked him. "Did we win?"

"Not yet," Raine answered. "Not ever, maybe. We won't know until we show up to start the trial. Either he will rule in our favor and we can all go home to get ready for the civil trial, or he will rule against us and we'll start picking a jury for the criminal case."

"That seems rather uncertain," Ophelia remarked.

"That's exactly what it is," Raine agreed. "But there is one thing that is certain."

"What's that?" Ophelia asked.

"I'm going to spend the next seven days getting ready to try this case," Raine said, "and win it."

21

Raine did in fact spend the entire following week preparing for Ophelia's criminal trial. It was true that they just couldn't do a civil case before a criminal case where the defendant had the right to remain silent. But in addition to that, the criminal case would give Raine a dry run at a lot of the witnesses who would also be testifying in the civil case. Except Porter. They'd lost a witness. But Raine had a replacement in mind.

"Finally," Sommers exclaimed Friday afternoon when they arrived at the Seattle Police downtown precinct. "I want to see what this Detective Gillespie has to say about Tommy."

Raine had asked her to spend a full day with him to go over everything before he entered the weekend, and kept working anyway. Sommers wasn't about to give up a full day to her side hustle, no matter how good she was getting at it, but she agreed to the afternoon. As long as the afternoon ended at 3:30. It was Friday, after all.

"Me too," Raine answered, "but let me do the talking. You're here as a witness to what he says, nothing more."

"I can't ask questions too?" Sommers pouted. "Why did you put Tommy in danger so that he was killed by some international drug cartel down on Pier 32?"

Raine held up in the middle of the lobby. "Now, see, that's exactly what I don't want us asking. Not today anyway."

"Why not?" Sommers protested. "That seems like the only question worth asking."

Raine shook his head. "No. The question is, how would a civilian like Kasaybian have access to the jail to kill Tommy? And if he didn't, then who would?"

Her eyes widened. "A detective."

Raine smiled darkly and nodded. "Follow my lead. Please."

"Absolutely," Sommers agreed with a salute, but it was earnest, not sarcastic.

Raine rolled his eyes slightly anyway and resumed the journey across the lobby to the reception desk. "We're here to see Detective Gillespie," he announced.

"Is he expecting you?" the officer at the reception desk asked. He was young, probably right out of the academy, with short hair and a baby face.

"No, but I think he'll want to see us," Raine answered. "Tell him there's an attorney here to talk to him about the death of Corrections Officer Kyle Porter. He'll know what that means."

"I know what that means," the officer answered. "That was just English, not a riddle or anything."

Raine offered a pained smile. "Can you just call him?"

The officer shrugged and picked up his telephone. "What's your name, sir?"

"Daniel Raine."

"And you're an attorney?"

"Yes, I am."

"That's too bad," the officer whispered under his breath, but Raine heard it anyway.

He looked to Sommers for support as the officer dialed the number.

But Sommers just shrugged. "A widely held opinion, I'm afraid."

Raine sighed. He supposed so, but he didn't understand why. He was just there to lie to a police officer to try to trick him into divulging confidential information that would help Raine's client but possibly endanger countless others. Then he understood a little bit why.

"Detective Gillespie won't see you," the officer informed them as he hung up the phone.

"Did you get a hold of him?" Raine asked.

"I did," the officer confirmed.

"Did you tell him it was about Officer Porter?" Raine followed up.

"I did," the officer said again.

"Did you tell him I was a lawyer?"

"I definitely did that," the officer answered. "That was when he said he wasn't going to talk to you."

"Ever?" Sommers interjected.

The officer shrugged. "We didn't get that specific. But definitely not today. And probably not tomorrow either, I would guess."

Raine stood there for a few moments, processing the situation. They had wanted to get some information from

Gillespie without giving up too much of their own information. His refusal to even see them was information in itself. And they had provided no information to him. Maybe it was a win after all.

"Thank you, young man." Raine waved a hand in the air. "You have been nominally helpful. You'll make an excellent police officer someday."

He guided Sommers away by the arm, and they huddled once outside the building.

"That was a bust," Sommers complained.

"For now," Raine answered, "but I'm a lawyer, remember?"

"You just said it, like, ten times," Sommers said.

"I did, didn't I?" Raine admitted. "Well, the thing about being a lawyer is that people don't get to just not answer my questions. They only get to choose the circumstances."

"What does that mean?" Sommers asked.

Raine answered her question with one of his own. "Have you ever served a subpoena?"

22

For Raine, the night before a trial was usually a time for reflection, considering the battle ahead, and finding peace in knowing that every preparation had been made. For Sawyer, she wanted to go out on one last date before he disappeared into back-to-back trials for a month or more. They compromised: takeout at Raine's place.

"You ready for tomorrow?" Sawyer asked him as they opened the bag of food the delivery person had left on Raine's welcome mat.

Raine nodded. "I think so. Except I don't even know what to expect. Taylor might dismiss the case and I'm done, or he might not and I'm going to start doing the things I've been prepping all week."

"It would almost be a shame if he did dismiss it," Sawyer said. "After all the work you put in."

"I want him to dismiss it," Raine made clear.

"Hey, I said 'almost.'" Sawyer laughed. She plopped down on Raine's couch. Even in a sweatshirt and yoga pants, she was stunning. "What are you going to do if he denies it? Appeal?"

Raine frowned. "I think that might be why he's waiting until the morning of the trial to reveal his ruling. Even if I immediately filed an appeal, the Court of Appeals won't stop a trial that's already started. They'll let the case play out. If I get an acquittal, there's nothing to appeal anyway. One less case for them."

"And if you lose the trial, you have a built-in appeal issue," Sawyer pointed out. "So that's something."

"Maybe I can get the Court of Appeals to declare that the prosecutor's office was vindictive," Raine reflected. "That would be more impressive anyway."

"And published in the case reports for everyone to see," she reminded him. "So just be sure to lose the motion and lose the trial so you can appeal. That should be easy."

"Easy?" Raine cocked his head at her. "You think I'm going to lose?"

"Note to self." Sawyer looked up and spoke into the air. "Night before trial, Dan has no sense of humor."

Raine frowned at her, which only proved her point.

"It was a joke, Dan," she said. "Of course I think you can win. But I also think you can lose. That's why you're wound up so tight tonight. You know that too."

Raine knew she was right. He took a deep breath. "Okay, I will try to relax tonight."

"Cool," Sawyer replied.

"And I will be more relaxed tomorrow morning," Raine continued, "knowing that even if I lose the motion and lose the trial, I already have an appeal issue."

Sawyer took a bite of her dinner and looked at him while she chewed. "That's a lie."

"That's a lie," Raine agreed. "I will be anything but relaxed tomorrow."

"Good." Sawyer leaned over and put her arm around him. "A really good lawyer I know once told me that if you're nervous, it means you're paying attention."

23

The morning of the trial, Raine was definitely not relaxed. But he was confident. Not confident they would win—that could never be guaranteed—but confident that he had done everything he could to be prepared. Ophelia Wilson was going to get his best.

They repeated their procedure from the previous Monday. They arrived fifteen minutes early, and Ophelia sat down with a legal pad that had nothing written on it except the word "Amen." Tennet arrived a few minutes later. No entourage that time. So they really had come to the motion hearing just to intimidate the judge. Raine shook his head slightly at the audacity.

The one difference was that Tennet and Raine didn't talk about the case before the judge came out. No last-minute begging to avoid the hearing.

Instead, the only conversation was Tennet being kind enough to tell Raine, "They reviewed your case. You're not going to be charged. You did a good job of following all the exceptions to prosecution."

Raine was relieved to hear that. He thanked her, and then they waited in silence until the judge appeared, accompanied by the bailiff's traditional bellow.

"Please be seated," Judge Taylor directed even before he himself had sat down atop the bench. He scanned the courtroom and frowned. "No audience today? Oh well, that is too bad. If anyone needs to hear what I have to say on this topic, it's probably the people here the other day."

Raine liked the sound of that. Maybe he'd be out of there by 9:15 after all.

"Are there any preliminary matters before I deliver my ruling?" the judge asked the attorneys.

Raine couldn't imagine what he or Tennet would possibly want to do before finding out whether they were going to have to do anything at all.

"No, Your Honor," Raine answered.

Tennet echoed his reply.

"All right then." Taylor pulled his reading glasses down from his bald head and began reading aloud. "In the matter of *The State of Washington versus Ophelia Wilson*, the defendant filed a motion to dismiss under the legal doctrine of vindictive prosecution..."

Raine leaned back into his chair. Some judges delivered their ruling immediately and succinctly. You knew immediately whether you had won or lost, and what the consequences were. Other judges delivered their rulings at the conclusion of oral arguments, but took their sweet time getting to the actual result, meandering first through a recitation of the facts, a summary of the arguments, and an analysis of the current state of the law before finally getting to the only thing the attorneys cared about: who won.

Then there was Judge Taylor. He waited a week to render

his decision, then presented it as a dramatic reading summarizing everything both attorneys already knew about the case.

"...formal criminal charges can only be brought in the superior court by the district attorney's office..."

Raine actually appreciated a judge who took their time and tried to do the right thing. That was his only real hope of winning. A shoot-from-the-hip judge would have dismissed his motion with the most minimal regard for the arguments, just because it was the safest thing to do.

"...the right to freedom of speech is protected by both the First Amendment to the United States Constitution and Article One, Section Five of the Washington State Constitution..."

Raine looked at his client. Ophelia had added a small doodle of an angel next to her "Amen" but no further words. Raine could hardly blame her. He was also having trouble listening to Judge Taylor read prepared remarks in a judicial monotone. He refocused on Taylor just as the judge was finally getting to the result.

"Ultimately, the decision I have to make is whether the King County Prosecutor's Office acted in bad faith when they filed the charges against Ms. Wilson. However, it is the potential bad faith by the law enforcement officers that gives me pause."

Raine frowned. He could finally see where it was going.

"I think it safe to say," Taylor continued, "that reasonable minds could differ about whether their actions against Ms. Wilson were truly necessary. The officers could simply have ignored Ms. Wilson until she became too tired, too cold, too hungry, too exhausted to carry on. Instead, they came at her in large numbers and used significant force to end her activities and remove her from her location. If there is any bad faith in this case, it is there.

"But once the decision to arrest Ms. Wilson was made, events unfolded. One of the officers said she scratched him. Another said she threatened him. Reports were filed with the prosecutor's office, and the prosecutors were under no obligation to ignore those reports.

"Do I think the police acted vindictively in retaliation for Ms. Wilson's exercise of her constitutional rights? Quite possibly. And I will look forward to seeing how that litigation turns out once it gets to a courtroom. But I do not believe I can transfer the police officers' vindictiveness to the prosecutor's office. It may have been a vindictive arrest, but it has not been proven that it was a vindictive prosecution. Accordingly, the defendant's motion to dismiss is denied."

Damn, Raine thought. But deep down, he had expected the result. He definitely did not expect what happened next.

"Thank you, Your Honor." Tennet stood to accept her victory. "The State has a motion."

"A motion?" Judge Taylor removed his reading glasses. "You won. What motion could you possibly have?"

"A motion to dismiss," Tennet answered, stone-faced. "This Court having ruled that our office did not engage in a vindictive prosecution against the defendant, now the State moves to dismiss the charges."

"All of them?" Taylor asked.

The judge was asking all the questions Raine wanted to ask. He also wanted Taylor to stop asking questions and just grant the motion. They could sort it out after the dismissal.

"Yes, Your Honor," Tennet confirmed with a crisp nod.

"Why?" Judge Taylor demanded. "And why did we go

through all of the trouble of the hearing on the defendant's motion if you were just going to dismiss anyway?"

"If the Court had ruled against us," Tennet explained, "my office would have appealed that ruling. Now that the Court has ruled in our favor, on balance, we would prefer to prevent any appeal of that ruling."

Taylor's eyebrows shot up. "You want to prevent Mr. Raine from appealing this ruling. You don't want the Court of Appeals overruling me and finding you were vindictive."

"On balance, my office believes this is the most satisfactory outcome of the criminal case against Ms. Wilson," Tennet answered without actually answering.

Judge Taylor stared at Tennet for several seconds, then laughed lightly and looked to Raine. "Any objection to the State's motion to dismiss, Mr. Raine?"

"Obviously not, Your Honor." Raine stood to reply. "I think I'm glad I lost my motion."

"I would think so too," Taylor agreed. "All right then. The State motion to dismiss is granted." A bang of the gavel. "Case dismissed."

"What just happened?" Ophelia asked. "Did we win?"

"We won," Raine confirmed. "I'm still not sure exactly how or why, but we won."

"Now what?" Ophelia asked.

There was always something next. "We get ready for the civil trial. Pierce is going to want to start it immediately. There's no way he didn't know Tennet was going to do that. That came from the highest levels. Which means he already has a day of preparation on me."

"That's bad," Ophelia said.

Raine patted her shoulder. "Don't worry about it. It's only

one day. They may have surprised us, but I've got a few surprises up my sleeve too."

24

As Raine expected, there was already an email from Jackson Pierce waiting for him when he got back to his office. Attached to the email was a scheduling order setting the first day of trial on the civil case for one week later. Another Monday start. That was the minimum amount of notice Pierce could give him under the court rules.

If he could have, Pierce would have walked into Taylor's courtroom and swapped places with Tennet, ready to start the civil trial there and then, and he wouldn't have spent the previous week distracted by a different, if related case. The criminal case had never been anything more than a way to delay the civil proceedings. That might not have been "vindictive," but it was certainly unseemly. He wondered if Tennet would get out of that closet-like office of hers now. Then he decided he didn't care after all. She'd played him. He wasn't going to let Pierce do the same.

Raine wished he could have had Judge Taylor again for the civil trial. He already knew the facts, and his ruling on the vindictive prosecution motion evidenced clear skepticism of law enforcement's motives when they tackled Ophelia in front of the building where they let her son die. But the judges rotated assignments based on the overall needs of the entire county court system. Judges were assigned to one of four divisions: criminal, civil, family, and juvenile. Taylor was in criminal. That meant he wouldn't be hearing the civil trial.

Instead the case was assigned to the newest judge on the Superior Court bench, Chloe Buxton-Greene.

Judge Buxton-Greene had been appointed to the Superior Court just a few months prior, when a position became open because the then-oldest judge on the bench had been forced to retire due to an unexpected, but overwhelming cascade of health problems. Buxton-Green had previously been a judge in the District Court, where simple misdemeanors and small claims cases were heard. She had gotten appointed to that position too, and no one was entirely sure why. Her application claimed several years of experience in criminal defense and family law, but no one had ever seen her in court, and most of the trial attorneys in the county met her for the first time when she stepped onto the bench in her brand-new judge's robe.

The good news was that she seemed to be a pretty good judge despite her apparent lack of experience. Not every referee had to play the game first, and ultimately that's all judges were: referees. The players were the trial attorneys. J. Daniel Raine. And Jackson Pierce.

Raine spent the week preparing even more for civil trial than he had spent preparing for the criminal trial the previous week, in large part because he had spent that previous week preparing for that criminal trial.

While Pierce had had inside knowledge that the criminal case would be dismissed to lock the vindictiveness ruling in appeal-proof amber, Raine had had to assume his client would be put in front of a jury who would decide whether to send her to prison for the next few years. Raine made no further attempts to speak with Detective Gillespie. He didn't have dinner with Sawyer.

And he most certainly didn't go back down to Pier 32. The last of the injuries to his face had finally healed. He didn't need fresh ones when he met the jurors for the first time on Monday morning.

———————

JUDGE BUXTON-GREENE'S courtroom was on the second floor of the courthouse, which was a kindness, as it meant no stairs or elevators.

The courthouse, like a substantial number of the buildings in downtown Seattle, was built into such a steep hill that there were two entrances on different floors. The doors to Third Avenue were on the first floor, and the doors to Fourth Avenue were on the second floor. In addition, the doors on the first floor were closed indefinitely due to the vandalism and hazardous waste conditions from the nearby homeless encampment, a decision finalized after one of the public defenders was assaulted in the stairwell by a transient man suffering a mental health episode.

Raine passed through security and headed directly to Judge Buxton-Greene's courtroom, where he found Ophelia waiting for him on a bench in the hallway.

"Are we ready?" Raine asked in his best life-coach voice.

Ophelia shrugged. "I think so. I'm still confused by what happened last week. Could that happen again today?"

Raine shook his head. "No, last week the plaintiff was the State of Washington, and the plaintiff can always dismiss their case. This week we're the plaintiffs, and I have no intention of dismissing our case."

Ophelia nodded. "Well, that's good. I'm glad I'm not going to jail."

Raine laughed. "I'm glad too."

"But I still miss Tommy."

Raine's jocularity vanished. It was good that she reminded him of the seriousness of the case for her. He cared too, but almost exclusively because he was getting paid to care. Even then, he cared about doing a good job. That would benefit Ophelia, but it was the sense of professional accomplishment that he would be chasing. That was fine, but he needed to make sure the jury didn't see that. They needed to see a lawyer personally invested in his client's suffering, like in that movie they'd seen a few years back, about that last honest lawyer and that desperate client who needed to sue somebody powerful, and win, against all odds. Raine nodded to himself. He could relate.

"I'm sure you do," he replied to his client. "Let's go inside and see if we can hold some people responsible."

Unlike Catherine Tennet, Jackson Pierce was already in the courtroom when Raine and Ophelia entered. By the looks of it, he'd been there for a while already. His table was covered in books and binders, and several easels were set up to the side of his counsel table, their display boards turned around to hide what was on them.

"Mr. Raine, good to see you again." Pierce strode over to shake his hand. "Please inform your client that my lack of greeting is not out of rudeness or animosity, but rather because our ethical rules prohibit speaking with a person we know is represented by another lawyer."

Raine looked at Ophelia and jabbed a thumb at Pierce. "What he said."

Ophelia offered a tight smile and a small nod. "Good morning, sir." Then she hurried to take a seat at the plaintiffs table. If she might have been confused by switching tables, Pierce's total takeover of the defendant's table left no room for her to sit there anyway.

"I can still offer that five-thousand-dollar settlement figure," Pierce said, definitely loudly enough for Ophelia to hear, ethical rules be damned. "We could both be out of here in time for lunch."

"Didn't you hear?" Raine replied. "I won my other case. I'm on a roll. I'm feeling good about my chances in this one too now."

Pierce smiled slyly at him. "I know all about what happened in your other case, and why. You lost your motion, and our boss got cold feet about the Court of Appeals reaching a different result and publishing it in the case reports. There's nothing in that which should give you a confidence boost about this case."

"I'll take what I can get." Raine wanted to keep it loose and low-key. He wanted Pierce to think he wasn't in the least worried about the trial. Whereas Pierce had obviously spent a great deal of time worrying about the trial. Raine nodded toward the easels and their secret placards. "What's with the easels? You have some exhibits you enlarged or something? Maybe a copy of Dr. Nieuwendyk's autopsy report where he wrote, 'I dunno'?"

"They are exhibits I intend to use at trial, yes," Pierce confirmed. "In my opening statement, in fact."

"Are you going to show them to me beforehand?" Raine asked.

"Not if I can avoid it," Pierce replied, "and not until the last possible moment."

Raine sighed. It was going to be like that. He had liked Pierce when they first met. He was buttoned-up with a confident energy. Now, Raine was finding it far less endearing. He hoped it would wear on the jury too.

"All rise!" shouted a bailiff, who had somehow entered the courtroom without Raine noticing. "The King County Superior Court is now in session, the Honorable Chloe Buxton-Greene presiding."

Judge Buxton-Greene walked leisurely to the bench and settled herself in before allowing, "You may be seated."

She was young, for a judge at least. Forty, at the most. With shiny black hair pulled back in a bun and smallish glasses perched on her nose.

"We are here on the matter of *Ophelia Wilson versus King County*," the judge read the case name from her printed calendar. "Are the parties all properly assembled?"

Raine was the plaintiff's attorney, so he got to go first this time. "Yes, Your Honor. Good morning. Daniel Raine appearing on behalf of the plaintiff, Ophelia Wilson, who is present and seated to my left."

Judge Buxton-Greene grunted slightly in acknowledgment, then turned to the other side.

"May it please the Court." Raine's opponent offered a deferential nod to the judge. "Jackson Pierce, on behalf of the defendant, King County."

"All right, good," Buxton-Greene said. She didn't seem to

actually be looking at either of them or anything in particular. She seemed to be squinting at something directly in front of her that was holding her attention, except that nothing was there. "Well, I want to get started as quickly as possible. We have a lot of cases in this courthouse, so I plan to use every minute of the day to get this case tried and completed as fast as possible so the next case can be assigned here."

Raine didn't make any response, as none seemed to be solicited.

"I'm going to seat twelve jurors and two alternate jurors," the judge continued. "You can each have two twenty-minute rounds to ask questions of the potential jurors. Challenges of a juror for cause should be made at the time the reason for the challenge becomes known. Peremptory challenges will be made out loud, in front of all the jurors."

Raine shared a glance with Pierce. He mirrored Raine's concerned expression. Usually, lawyers preferred to strike jurors on paper or at sidebar so the remaining jurors wouldn't know which side booted which juror. Also usually, judges took input from the lawyers about how to try the case, rather than be quite so obvious about dictating every detail from the bench.

"Your Honor," Raine interrupted, "could the lawyers perhaps be heard regarding the number of alternate jurors, or the length of our questioning, or how peremptory challenges are made?"

Buxton-Greene finally looked directly at Raine.

He realized that he preferred it when she wasn't really looking at anything.

"Did you not hear what I said when I started speaking, counsel?" she asked. "I said that we will try this case in an efficient and expedient manner. I have enough experience to know how many alternate jurors to seat, and to know that attorneys will take hours, even days, to speak to prospective jurors if given the chance. No, I am comfortable in running my courtroom in the way that I believe works best for the administration of justice and individual litigants, even if the attorneys for those litigants may feel a bit stifled."

Raine looked again at Pierce, but his expression had shifted markedly, and he was looking again at the judge.

"The defendant has no objections or concerns about any of the Court's directives, Your Honor," he ingratiated. "Thank you for explaining them to us so thoroughly."

Raine shook his head at Pierce's change of attitude, but only slightly so the judge wouldn't notice it. She didn't seem like she would appreciate emoting by the attorneys.

"Mr. Pierce, I see you have commandeered the easels from the back of the courtroom," Judge Buxton-Greene remarked.

"Yes, Your Honor," Pierce replied. "I have several exhibits that—"

"Do not move court property without first asking permission," the judge interrupted. "Whatever those are, you will not use them in opening statement. I will not risk a mistrial because you showed a picture to the jury in opening statement, then failed to have it admitted at trial."

"I can assure you, Your Honor, that I know how to admit an exhibit at trial," Pierce protested.

"And I can assure you that you don't admit exhibits," the judge retorted. "I do. You make a motion to admit, but then I decide whether to grant that motion. You will not use those exhibits in your opening statement."

Raine felt better. Now they both had gotten in trouble.

Plus, he wouldn't have to argue about Pierce using the exhibits in his opening statement.

"Speaking of opening statements," the judge continued, "they will be limited to twenty minutes. I used to allow thirty minutes, but there's no story that can't be told in twenty minutes."

Raine considered arguing again. He didn't want any time limit on his opening statement. Every story was different, and every story took as long as it took to tell. Artificial time constraints were not, in his opinion, consistent with effective advocacy or the just results that were supposed to come out of such adversarial advocacy. On the other hand, he had no reason to believe he would change the judge's mind.

Judge Buxton-Greene rattled off a series of further instructions and directives, concerning everything from the hours court would be in session (Monday through Friday, 9:00 a.m. to 5:00 p.m.), to what sorts of drinks would be allowed on the counsel tables (water only, no coffee, and absolutely no soft drinks).

Raine's initial annoyance at being controlled slowly gave way to an appreciation of the judge's efficiency. It took the entire day, but by the end of it, all preliminary matters had been addressed, and the jury had been selected, seated, and sworn in.

Judge Buxton-Greene then adjourned the trial until 9:00 a.m. the next morning. And once everyone was assembled in her courtroom, the judge looked down at the fourteen jurors seated obediently in the jury box. "We will now begin the trial. Ladies and gentlemen, please give your attention to Mr. Raine, who will deliver the opening statement on behalf of the plaintiff."

25

Raine stood up, buttoned his suitcoat, and stepped out from behind the counsel table. He nodded to the judge but eschewed the overly formal, "May it please the Court." It was Old Lawyerese, and if he spoke it, he would other himself, acknowledging, even flaunting, a distinction between himself and the jurors. He wanted the jurors to trust him, and it can be hard to trust people who are other.

He took up the same spot he always took to deliver an opening statement: dead center of the jury box, close enough to telegraph confidence but not so close as to invade anyone's personal space. He rooted his feet to that spot so he wouldn't pace and clasped his hands in front of himself, a gesture of sincerity and one that kept him from talking too much with his hands. He was ready to speak, and everyone in the courtroom was waiting on his next word.

The problem Raine faced was that opening statement was supposed to be a summary of what the lawyer expected the evidence to show. Basically the story that would be pieced together by the question-and-answer sessions of each witness, along with those giant photos or whatever they were that Pierce had, and any other exhibits. Evidence usually came in piecemeal over the course of a trial, with interruptions for objections or lunch or even another witness whose schedule doesn't allow them to wait until the afternoon. Opening statement was the first and only time the jury would hear the full story, beginning to end, in a way that was understandable, compelling, and persuasive. That's what opening statement was supposed to be.

But Raine couldn't tell the jury what had happened to Tommy Wilson. Because he didn't actually know what had happened to Tommy Wilson. Not yet. But if things went as planned, the jury would forgive him for not giving the opening statement he wanted to give: Detective Gillespie was running Tommy as a confidential informant, trying to expose the drug operation running through Axis Global, but Tommy's cover got blown, and he knew too much.

The only thing Raine wasn't sure about was whether Kasaybian had paid off the guard to get to Tommy, or Gillespie had done it with his badge. That would come out when Gillespie testified. He could refuse to answer Raine's questions at the precinct, but he couldn't refuse to answer them in the courtroom after being served with a subpoena. And when Raine finally had him on his turf, the truth would come out.

But not until then. If Raine said it to the jury now, Pierce would say it to Gillespie at the first break. No, he needed to keep it to himself so Gillespie wouldn't see it coming. But that meant Raine didn't have a story to tell in his opening. So he leaned into it to make it a strength.

"Tommy Wilson is dead." Good attention-grabber, what

trial lawyers called the first sentence of their opening state-ment. Simple, yet important.

"And nobody knows why." Even more attention-grabbing.

"Or rather"—Raine raised one hand and pointed a finger to the ceiling—"no one will say why."

And suddenly a lack of information became a conspir-acy. And most conspiracies are fed by a lack of information. The lack of information itself is what proves the conspiracy. Circular but impenetrable logic. But the jury would need a few more details.

"Let's back up." Raine lowered his hand again. "Let's start with Tommy Wilson. Let me tell you a little bit about Tommy, because he's the reason we're all here today. His death is the reason we're all here."

Raine opened his stance and gestured toward his client. "I think the best way to introduce Tommy is to introduce his mother, Ophelia."

Ophelia started to make a halting wave at the jurors, but then stopped, clearly unsure whether she was allowed. A couple of the jurors did the same thing.

Raine could have warned Ophelia he was going to do that, but he wanted the jurors to see a genuine and vulner-able reaction. He wanted them to see she was a regular person, just like them. Awkward and uncomfortable in a courtroom. But Raine loved being in a courtroom.

"Ophelia is forty-six years old. She was born and raised right here in Seattle. She went to Garfield High and lives in Columbia City, what we used to call Rainier Valley."

Seattle could be an insular place. Native Seattleites were far outnumbered by transplants from California and the

Midwest. If there were any natives on the jury, they would appreciate a fellow Rain City native.

"She works as a medical records technician up on First Hill." More local nomenclature. "She takes her dog for walks around Green Lake, and she likes to spend Sunday mornings at the Fremont Farmer's Market."

Okay, that was enough. Ophelia was one of us, one of them. Time to move along. Especially with only twenty minutes to talk.

"She had one child." Raine allowed a pained expression to cross his face. "Tommy. She raised Tommy by herself. Tommy's dad was never really in his life. But he was Ophelia's whole life. But as anyone with kids will tell you, you're not usually their whole life. And kids will do things that hurt you, that hurt themselves. Tommy was a good kid, but I'm not going to stand up here and tell you that he was an angel. He wasn't. He was an addict. As anyone with a loved one who's an addict will tell you, the drugs become that person's whole life. And so it was for Tommy." A raised finger again. "For a while."

Another glance back at his client. "But Ophelia was always there for him, even as he started getting arrested and even as he would go dark for days at a time. She was always there for him. She wanted him to quit, but it's not as easy as just that. That's why it's called an addiction. Tommy the rebellious teenager grew into Tommy the struggling young adult. He found jobs here and there, mostly retail and food service. Enough to pay his rent, and the drugs if he was using just then.

"He wanted to quit too. His life wasn't better for the drugs. But every now and again, they helped make a day a little better, a little easier. At least until he got arrested again or fired because he slept through his shift. But through it all, Ophelia was there for him, and every time he said he wanted to quit, she helped get him into treatment. Even if it was only for one day, she took him, and she paid for it, and she was ready to do it as many times as it took.

"Until there weren't any more times. Because Tommy was gone." Raine took a moment to let his words so far sink in.

He took a deep cleansing breath, then continued, "You probably think that I'm going to tell you that Tommy overdosed. That he died in a gutter somewhere down in Pioneer Square, and now Ophelia is suing the county because she blames the cops and firefighters for not saving him."

There were a couple of nods from the jury box.

"Well, that's not what happened. In fact, the doctor who performed the autopsy on Tommy will tell you that he definitely did not die of a drug overdose. He did have trace amounts of drugs in his blood, but nothing that would even make him high, let alone kill him. No, not only will the doctor tell you drugs didn't kill Tommy, he's going to tell you he doesn't know what killed Tommy Wilson."

If Raine was going to lean into the lack of information in the case, this was where he was going to lean the most.

"The doctor's name is Peter Nieuwendyk, and he has one job. His job is to conduct autopsies on dead bodies and determine what killed them. That's what he does. He went to college and medical school and did several different residencies to end up becoming what is called a forensic pathologist. Pathology is things that are wrong with the body, and forensic means, well, you know. It means following clues and discovering the truth. Dr. Nieuwendyk's one job is to determine how people died, but the only thing he's going to be able to tell you is what it wasn't. It wasn't a gunshot wound. It wasn't blunt force trauma. And it wasn't drugs."

Raine relaxed his hands again and raised one of them about chest level to point, loosely, at the jury box. "He won't be able to tell you what happened. And he works for the defendant, King County. You're going to see a pattern with that."

Raine took another breath and reset his body positioning. Then he continued, "Now sometimes, it's possible to determine how someone died from the scene of their death. If someone steps in front of a speeding truck, it probably won't take a forensic pathologist to tell you how he died. So, what was the scene like where Tommy died?"

Raine threw his hands up. "Again, no one knows. Or they won't say. But to fully understand where Tommy died and why that is the fault of King County, we need to back up a few hours on the morning he died."

Tommy getting arrested was not a great fact for Raine. Jurors were usually law-abiding citizens who expected others to also abide by the law. They actually responded to their jury summons. There was a real risk that some of the jurors would discount the value of Tommy's life because of his criminal history, even if it arose out of an addiction. On the other hand, there was no way around the fact that Tommy died in the county jail. That was why they were suing the county.

"Again, details are few and far between," Raine warned. "We know that Tommy was booked into the King County Jail shortly after midnight. He was booked on a single count of possession of a controlled substance. The booking roster doesn't even say which substance it was. But we do know he wasn't actually using that night because his levels were too low for that. So a sober Tommy Wilson was booked into the King County Jail for allegedly possessing an unspecified, unknown controlled substance."

Raine shook his head slightly and shrugged. "I wish I could tell you Tommy wasn't still using drugs at that time of his life. I wish he'd never been arrested, and I wish he'd never been booked into the county jail. But the reason I wish that isn't because he had relapsed again. It's because Tommy walked into the jail that night, but he never walked out again. He died while in the custody and care of the King County Jail." Time to raise his voice. "And no one knows why!"

The raised voice had its desired effect. If anyone had started dozing off, they were awake again. And all of the jurors had just received a shot of adrenaline that would help them not just hear Raine's words, but feel them.

"Or no one will say why," Raine posited. "Here's what we do know. He was booked into jail shortly after midnight. He was placed into solitary confinement at 12:30 a.m. And he was found dead in his cell at approximately 5:20 a.m. That's it. That's what we know. That's what they're telling us. He was just dead. And no one, not even the medical examiner, knows why."

Raine shook his head, slowly at first, then faster and stronger. "That is not acceptable. And it is not enough to avoid liability in this case. The county, through its employees and its jail, has an obligation to care for the people in its custody. Remember, this isn't a situation where Tommy checked into a seedy motel in the bad part of town and is complaining he got bed bugs. Tommy didn't choose to go to the King County Jail that night. In fact, I'm sure if he had been given the choice, he would have gone anywhere but there. But the county, through its employees and its jail, forced Tommy to spend the night there. And when they did that, they took on the responsibility of, at a bare minimum, keeping him alive."

Raine turned back again, but looked at Pierce this time. He shook his head in disappointment, then turned back to the jurors. "Now, when I finish speaking with you, Mr. Pierce is going to stand up and deliver his opening statement. I expect him to say something along the lines of, 'If we don't know what happened, then the plaintiff didn't meet their burden of proof.' And I will agree that Ms. Wilson and I have the burden of proof in this case, but we will meet that burden. And to the extent that the full story hasn't been told because the county's own agents and employees are hiding the truth—well, that just meets that burden even more."

Time to wrap up. Raine had kept one eye on the clock on the courtroom wall. He'd been talking for nineteen minutes. He had no doubt Buxton-Greene would interrupt him mid-sentence precisely at the twenty-minute mark.

"So, ladies and gentlemen, after you've heard all of the evidence—and seen what evidence is missing and why—we believe you will be more than convinced that King County should be held liable for the wrongful death of Tommy Wilson. Thank you."

Raine turned and walked back to his seat. He glanced up at the judge and noted that she seemed disappointed she hadn't been able to cut him off. Maybe Pierce would go over time.

"Now, ladies and gentlemen," Judge Buxton-Greene announced, "please give your attention to Mr. Pierce, who will deliver the opening statement on behalf of the defendant."

Pierce stood up and stepped out from behind his counsel table. His suit was in perfect order, and he held himself with obvious confidence. "Thank you, Your Honor. May it please the court." He stepped over to the jury box and stood almost exactly where Raine had stood, except a half step closer to the jury box.

A good adjustment, Raine thought, since he was on defense. It would communicate increased urgency, but without getting too close to the jurors. A full step would have been too much.

"Not everything happens for a reason," Pierce began. "And not everything can be blamed on someone else. Sometimes bad things happen, and no one did anything to make it happen. It's hard to accept, especially if you're the one who the bad thing happened to, but it's the truth, and this is a courtroom, so we must deal with truth. We must face it. We must accept it. And we must speak it."

He leaned back that half-step and settled into the neutral position that Raine had staked out. He was done with his attention-grabber. Now he would provide his explanation, a more cerebral exercise that called for a less aggressive posture.

"Mr. Raine and I agree on several things," Pierce said. "In fact, I would guess that we agree on almost everything in this case. Except what conclusion can and should be drawn from it. This isn't a case where dueling pathologists give different opinions as to the cause of death. This isn't a situation where a wild, out-of-control situation led to someone being trampled to death, and every witness has a different memory of what took place.

"No, the facts in this case are simple. Mr. Wilson committed a crime. He was arrested for that crime, which is what the community expects to happen. He was booked into the county jail, which again is what we as a community expect when someone breaks the law. Then, for reasons unknown, Mr. Wilson passed away in his cell. That's what happened. That's all that happened. And that is not enough to hold the county liable for wrongful death. You will hear from a series of corrections officers and other county employees, and they will tell you that all standard procedures were followed that night. What more can we do?"

Pierce frowned slightly and turned to cast a sympathetic eye on Ophelia Wilson. "It's a tragedy to lose someone close to you, especially a child. And it's understandable to want to find someone to blame and make them pay."

He turned back to the jurors. "But nothing that happens in this courtroom over the course of this trial will bring back Tommy Wilson. Not even placing blame on people who did nothing wrong. When this trial concludes, you will not have heard sufficient evidence to prove King County is in any way liable for the tragic and untimely death of Tommy Wilson. That is the truth. And no matter how much you might sympathize with Ms. Wilson, it will be your duty to speak that truth. Thank you."

Pierce didn't even come close to the twenty-minute mark. Raine avoided looking at the judge lest she decide to place time limits on the witnesses too. Because that was what was next.

"Mr. Raine," Judge Buxton-Green called down, "you may call your first witness."

Raine stood. "Thank you, Your Honor. We call Ophelia Wilson to the stand."

26

O phelia stood up, and Raine directed her to stand in front of the judge to be sworn in.

"Raise your right hand," Buxton-Green instructed. "Do you solemnly swear or affirm that the testimony you give in this proceeding will be the truth, the whole truth, and nothing but the truth?"

Ophelia nodded, hand raised. "I do."

"Please take the witness stand." The judge pointed to the chair on the raised platform attached to the side of the judicial bench. Then, to Raine, "Whenever you're ready, counsel."

Ophelia was the logical first witness. Not only did she have the most information about Tommy, but she was the emotional center of the case. It was she who'd lost her child, her one and only child. And it was also she who would receive any award the jury awarded in its verdict—minus Raine's forty percent. Raine would focus on the former. He knew Pierce would address the latter.

"Please state your name for the record," Raine began the examination.

"Ophelia Marie Wilson." She seemed uncertain where to look when she gave her answer.

Raine had instructed her to turn and deliver her answer to the jury—they liked that—but it was a very unnatural way to have a conversation.

"How old are you, Ms. Wilson?" Raine tried to coach her with a dart of his eyes toward the jury box.

"I'm forty—" She started to speak to Raine, then turned to the jurors. "I'm forty-six. Sorry, I'm a little nervous."

Raine scanned the jury box for their reaction. One or two smiled back, but most kept their poker faces. They had a job to do too, and they were taking it seriously. It would be unprofessional to show favoritism so early in the case.

"Are you employed?"

"Yes." Again she started talking to Raine, then turned to the jurors. "I work at PrimaClinic at Ninth and James. I'm a medical records technician."

"How long have you been a medical records technician at PrimaClinic?" Raine asked.

It was all background to start, but it helped the jury get to know Ophelia a little better, and it helped her get comfortable on the stand, which would be important when they started talking about Tommy. So, Ophelia detailed a bit of her work history. How many years she'd worked there. What she'd done before she was promoted to medical records technician. Where she worked before that. Basically she was a good worker who had spent most of her career in and around health care.

"Is there a reason you've spent most of your career in the health care field?" Raine asked.

Ophelia thought for a moment, then sighed slightly. "There are two reasons, actually. The first is that I love helping people."

"And what's the second?"

"The second reason is that I needed to make sure I had good health benefits," Ophelia told the jurors. "For Tommy."

And they were off to the races.

"Why did you need to have good health benefits for Tommy?" Raine asked. He had kind of already told everyone in his opening statement, but opening statements weren't evidence. They were just lawyers talking. He needed a witness to say it under oath.

"Tommy had a drug problem," Ophelia answered with less emotion than Raine might have preferred. He supposed she had told people that countless times over the last decade or so. It would lose its impact eventually. "My insurance paid for treatment."

"Did he do substance abuse recovery treatment?" Raine asked hopefully.

"Oh, yes." Ophelia laughed lightly. "He did it a whole bunch of times. Because it never took."

"What kind of drugs did he use?" Raine figured the jury would be curious, and it was never a good idea to leave the jurors curious.

"Well, I can't say for sure because he never did them with me," Ophelia answered. "But from what he told me and what the counselors were allowed to tell me, he was addicted to opioids and also used cocaine, methamphetamine, and a few other things. Oh, and marijuana, of course, but that's legal now, so I don't know if it counts."

"What about any of the newer drugs?" Raine decided to ask. "Ketamine? Fentanyl?"

Ophelia shrugged. "I don't really know what those are."

Raine supposed that was a good thing.

"When was the last time you saw Tommy?" Raine moved on. "And to the best of your knowledge, was he using drugs at that time?"

"I saw him two days before he died," Ophelia answered, her voice breaking on the last word. "I don't know if he was using then. He was sober when he was with me. He was almost always sober when he was with me."

Again, jurors might be curious. "Almost always?" Raine asked.

"There were a couple of times when he came to me because he was using and he needed help," Ophelia recalled. She looked at the ceiling and brushed at the corners of her welling eyes. "There were a couple of times when I thought he was going to die. When he was just as helpless as the first day I held him. And just like then, I took care of him. I took care of my baby. I got him to the doctor, and I got him into rehab. He may have relapsed later, but he didn't die that night, I'll tell you that."

Raine was getting to see a side of Ophelia she had kept hidden in their consultations. She had always deferred to him. He didn't notice anything unusual. He was the lawyer, giving her advice. It was the nature of the relationship. But now he was seeing the strong independent woman she had to be to raise a drug-addicted son on her own. Her Mama Bear was coming out, and Raine liked it. He suspected the jury did too.

"If he had come to you that last time, two days before he died, and he had been high like those other times," Raine asked, "what would you have done?"

"I would have taken him to the doctor and taken him to

rehab until he was sober enough to walk out again. I would have done that a hundred times. I probably did do it a hundred times. I'd have done it a thousand times. A million times."

"So let me ask you this, Ms. Wilson." Raine leaned in slightly and opened his stance to the jury. "What would you have done the night he died if you could have been there for him?"

That did it. The tears that she had been holding back poured down the outsides of her cheeks, and a sob escaped from her chest. "Anything! I would have done anything! He was my little boy. My little boy. I would have done anything!"

"And what would you expect the personnel at the county jail to have done to help him?"

She thought for a moment, her eyes red and her cheeks glistening. "Something. They should have done something. Anything."

Raine had considered asking Ophelia about her arrest a few days later. He knew it would draw an objection from Pierce, and a reasonable one at that. It would be a lengthy argument, and the judge would probably have the jury go to the jury room until they worked it out.

Raine would argue that the officers' actions against Ophelia showed a guilty conscious regarding their responsibility for Tommy's death. Pierce would argue that it occurred days later, it had nothing to do with whatever steps the jail staff did or didn't or should or shouldn't have taken, and anyway Ophelia was the one who'd committed the crimes. That would lead to another argument about whether the jury would get to hear that Ophelia was charged with crimes, and if so, whether they would get to know when and how the criminal case was dismissed. It could take an hour or more while the jury sat in their soundproof room and wondered what was going on.

Or he could end his direct examination on an emotionally charged high note and dare Pierce to cross-examine a crying mother.

"No further questions, Your Honor," Raine announced, and he returned to his seat.

All eyes, including Ophelia's wet ones, turned to Jackson Pierce.

He stood but didn't even come out from behind the defense table. "The only question I might have posed was to ask whether Ms. Wilson was present at the time of her son's unfortunate passing," he declared, ostensibly to the judge but truly for the jury to hear, "but I believe she has already testified convincingly that she was not. Accordingly, Your Honor, I have no questions for this witness. Thank you."

He sat down again, and Raine could only appreciate Pierce's wise choice not to badger a crying woman whose son had died, regardless of the circumstances. He had asked his question without actually asking it, and looked like a gentleman doing it. *Bravo.*

"You are excused from the witness stand," Judge Buxton-Greene barked suddenly. "You may return to your seat at the plaintiff's table."

Ophelia jumped at the sound of the judge's voice, then nodded meekly and made her way from the witness stand to sit down again next to Raine.

"We will now take our morning recess," the judge announced. "We will reconvene in fifteen minutes. Be prepared to call your next witness, Mr. Raine."

He was prepared all right. The rest of the witnesses were going to be far more hostile than Ophelia.

27

"The plaintiff calls Officer Scott Park to the stand," Raine announced once everyone was reassembled in Judge Buxton-Greene's courtroom.

The jurors turned to watch a uniformed Seattle police officer enter the courtroom and approach the judge to be sworn in. He was average height and build, with short black hair and a clean-shaven face. Typical cop.

"Please state your name for the record," Raine began the examination.

"Scott Park." He knew to turn and deliver his answers to the jury. They taught that at the academy.

"How are you employed, sir?"

"I'm a police officer with the Seattle Police Department." Obvious from his uniform, but he still needed to say it for the record.

"How long have you been a police officer with Seattle?" Raine asked the next background question.

"It'll be three years next month," he told the jurors with a warm grin. He seemed to be a likable fellow.

"Did you have any law enforcement experience prior to starting at Seattle PD?"

"Yes," Park answered. "I was an officer with the Issaquah Police Department for just over a year prior to being hired by Seattle."

"Okay, thank you." Raine signaled the end of the résumé questions. "What are your current job title and duties?"

"I'm a patrol officer," Park told the jury. "I work swing shift, which for us is eighteen-hundred hours to zero-two-hundred hours."

"Six p.m. to two a.m.?" Raine translated for the jurors.

"Yes," Park agreed with a nod.

"What do you do during your shift?"

"General patrol," Park answered. "Proactive policing and responding to calls."

"What's proactive policing?" Raine asked.

"That's where I'm looking for illegal activity myself," Park explained. "I see something myself and take actions to address it myself. For example, I might see a car weaving across the lane divider, so I pull them over and begin a DUI investigation."

"What about responding to calls?" Raine followed up.

Park nodded and turned to the jurors again. "That's when dispatch puts out a call for officers to respond to a crime reported by a citizen, usually by calling 911. If I'm in the vicinity, I will respond to the scene and advise dispatch I'm on my way."

"And you do that for eight straight hours every night?" Raine asked.

"More like seven," Park answered. "I have to get my paperwork finished before I sign off. They don't want to pay us for writing reports."

"Of course not," Raine agreed. "Because your job is chasing bad guys, right?"

Park shrugged slightly. "I'm not sure that's how I'd put it."

"But that's part of it, right?" Raine pressed. "Isn't that part of why people want to become police officers? To chase the bad guys?"

"Some guys," Park allowed. "Some of us want to help the community. Chasing bad guys is one way of doing that."

"Did you have occasion to chase a bad guy by the name of Tommy Wilson?" Raine moved on to the case at hand.

Park nodded. "Yes, sir."

"And to be clear"—Raine raised a hand slightly toward the officer—"you probably wouldn't have remembered Mr. Wilson except for the fact that you knew you were going to testify here today, is that right?"

Park thought for a moment. "I think that's probably fair. I interact with a lot of people every night. I had to look up my report before testifying today to really be able to remember anything."

"And what do you remember about your interaction with Mr. Wilson?"

"I arrested him." Simple enough.

"For what?" Raine asked.

"Possession of a controlled substance," Park answered. Then he translated it himself. "Drug possession."

"Do you recall which drug it was?" Raine asked.

Park thought again, then shook his head slightly. "I think the dispatch was for heroin, but when I got there, it was something different. Pills, I think?"

"So you were dispatched? You didn't come across Tommy yourself, shooting up on a street corner or something?"

"No, I was definitely dispatched," Park answered. "It's hard to just see someone possessing drugs."

"Why is that?" Raine prompted.

"Well, for one thing, drug addicts usually try to hang out in places they won't be seen by cops," was the answer.

"So you knew Tommy was an addict?" Raine challenged.

"Well," Park hesitated, "he was using, so I would guess he was probably addicted."

"But you don't know him from prior arrests or anything, do you?"

"Oh, no," Park agreed. "He wasn't someone I had arrested a bunch of times for drug possession, no. I was just dispatched to the corner of Fourth and Cherry, and I found him, and I arrested him."

"Were the drugs in open view when you arrived?" Raine inquired. "Or did you find them pursuant to a search?"

Park rubbed his chin. "I don't think they were out in the open when I arrived. They usually aren't." He pointed to his attire. "I wear a uniform and drive a marked car. By the time I get out of the car, most people notice I'm a police officer."

"Did Tommy notice that?" Raine followed up.

Another hand to the chin. "You know, he sort of didn't. He already seemed pretty out of it when I arrived. He was definitely under the influence of something. That's why I searched his bag."

"Without a warrant?" Raine questioned.

"A search incident to arrest is an exception to the warrant requirement," Park returned, and correctly.

"True," Raine allowed, "but what was he under arrest for?"

"Possession of a controlled substance," Park repeated. "I already told you that."

"But how did you search his bag incident to arrest for possession of a controlled substance," Raine challenged, "if you didn't find the controlled substance until you searched the bag?"

Park frowned. "He was obviously under the influence of something."

"So public intoxication?" Raine suggested.

"Sure," Park agreed.

"Public intoxication isn't a crime in Washington," Raine informed him, "unless you're underage. Tommy was over twenty-one, correct?"

Park sighed. "Look, I know I arrested him for possession of a controlled substance, I know he was in possession of a controlled substance, and he sure seemed to be under the influence of a controlled substance. It was a pretty simple callout, no matter how complicated you're trying to make it now."

Raine nodded. "That's fair. Who called the police?"

"What?" Park asked.

"Who called 911 to report that Tommy Wilson was in possession of a controlled substance on a downtown street corner at midnight?"

"I have no idea," Park admitted.

"Because dispatch doesn't tell you the identity of the caller?" Raine suggested.

"No, because it was an anonymous tip," Park answered. "I remember that because usually when it's an anonymous tip, there's nothing there when you arrive. I was actually surprised to see anyone on that corner at all, let alone someone who matched the description."

"So there was a description of the suspect?" Raine asked.

"I mean, just the basics," Park answered. "Race and sex, general clothing."

"And Tommy matched the description?"

"He did, yes," Park answered. "It was him."

Raine took a moment. He'd set the stage for what really mattered in the case: what happened at the jail. And he'd rattled Park at least a little bit. It was good for the jurors to see law enforcement could make mistakes. That was the basis of his entire case.

"What did you do after you arrested him?" Raine continued.

"I transported him to the King County Jail," Park answered.

"Only a block away," Raine pointed out.

"Two," Park argued. "One up to Fifth and one over to James."

"Okay," Raine allowed. "What did you do when you got there?"

"I booked him on one count of a controlled substance."

"Pills, probably?" Raine asked again.

"I believe so," Park answered. "The most common drug we see in pill form is fentanyl, but there's no preliminary presumptive test for that yet. You have to send it to the crime lab. I think that's why I can't say for sure what substance it was now."

"Did he seem to be under the influence of fentanyl?" Raine asked.

"I'm not a drug recognition expert," Park demurred. "I applied for that training last year, but I wasn't accepted. I'm going to try again this year."

"I'm sure this case will help your career, Officer Park,"

Raine said grimly. "I don't think I have any more questions for you at this time."

But he did. That was why he didn't say the formal "no further questions." He took a few steps toward his counsel table even as Pierce began to stand up. Then he turned around with a finger raised toward the ceiling. "Oh, I do have one more question. Mr. Wilson never assaulted you in any way, right?"

"Assaulted me?" Park repeated back. "No. No, not that I recall."

"And you would recall that, wouldn't you?" Raine wanted a definitive response.

"Yes, I think I would have recalled that," Park admitted.

"Thank you, Officer." With that, Raine was ready to say it. "No further questions."

Pierce had remained standing for Raine's dramatic "one more question." He waited for Raine to actually sit down before coming out from behind his table.

"Hello, Officer Park," he greeted the witness warmly. Why not? They were on the same team. "Thank you for coming here today."

Park shrugged. "I got a subpoena."

"Of course you did," Pierce responded. "Well, I only have a few questions for you, so you should be finished with your obligations under that subpoena very shortly."

"Sounds good," Park replied.

"Did Mr. Wilson appear to be in any medical distress during your contact with him?"

"No," Park answered. "He seemed intoxicated, but not in any distress."

"Intoxicated how?" Pierce asked.

"Slow, lethargic," Park answered. "I had to repeat myself several times."

"Did he have any trouble standing or walking?"

"A little," Park answered, "but it seemed more cognitive than physical. He was just sort of out of it."

"And, Officer, if he had been in any sort of medical distress," Pierce continued, "you would have called for paramedics to examine him on the spot, wouldn't you?"

"Absolutely," Park assured the jurors solemnly. "Any time we observe a suspect experience medical issues, we stop the arrest process and call for medical."

"And you didn't need to do that for Mr. Wilson, correct?" Pierce asked the same question yet again.

"Correct," Park confirmed, yet again.

"Lastly, I want to address Mr. Raine's final questions to you." Pierce signaled. "As you sit here today, you don't recall Mr. Wilson assaulting you, is that correct?"

"That is correct," Park agreed.

"But if the corrections staff recalled you saying something about Mr. Wilson being combative," Pierce basically told him what to say, "that would probably be because something did happen and you just don't remember it here and now. Is that fair to say?"

Park took a moment to answer. "I mean. Yes, I guess so. If they remember me saying that, I suppose I must have had a reason."

"I'm sure you did," Pierce replied. "Thank you, Officer Park. No further questions." Pierce returned to his seat.

Judge Buxton-Greene looked down at Raine. "Any redirect examination based on the cross-examination?"

Raine stood up. "Yes, Your Honor." He didn't bother stepping out from behind his table. "You say you must have had a reason to report Mr. Wilson was combative. But you don't actually remember any such reason now, do you? Even after Mr. Pierce basically told you to say you did."

"Objection!" Pierce bolted to his feet.

"Sustained," Buxton-Greene ruled without hearing any response from Raine. "You will not impugn the integrity of opposing counsel in my courtroom, Mr. Raine."

"Of course not, Your Honor," Raine replied. "I withdraw the question."

He turned back to Park and asked the same question in a different way. "You seem like someone who appreciates the responsibility that comes with being a police officer and wants to do the right thing, Officer Park. So I'll just ask it as plainly as I can. Mr. Wilson wasn't combative with you, was he?"

Park took a deep breath, held it, then exhaled and shook his head. "No. Not that I remember."

That was as good as Raine was going to get. "Thank you, Officer. No further questions."

Pierce didn't ask to conduct recross-examination. Jurors hated a tennis-match-like back-and-forth over the same question. Park was excused, and Raine called his next witness.

"The plaintiff calls William Frazier to the stand."

Corrections Officer Frazier entered the courtroom. If he had seemed upset about appearing for the earlier deposition, he appeared downright angry as he marched to the bench to be sworn in. His face was already red, and when he sat down on the witness stand, he locked eyes with Raine, like he was trying to stare a hole into the back of Raine's head.

Raine wasn't in the least fazed. "Please state your name for the record," he began nonchalantly.

"William Alexander Frazier." It was almost a growl.

"How are you employed, sir?"

"I am a corrections officer at the King County Correctional Facility." He didn't turn to deliver his answers to the jury. As a corrections officer, he probably hadn't been to the police academy. Besides, it would have meant taking his bulging eyes off Raine.

"That's what everybody else calls the King County Jail, right?" Raine tried to translate for the jury.

"I don't know what everybody else calls it," Frazier replied through his set jaw. "It's the King County Correctional Facility."

"Okay, that's fine." He didn't mind Frazier being hostile. It supported the theme of his entire case. "Let's just get right to it, shall we? You were on duty the night Tommy Wilson died, is that correct?"

"It was the morning," Frazier argued, "and yes."

"The morning," Raine repeated. "Because it happened between midnight and, what time again? When was Mr. Wilson's body found?"

"Zero-five-twenty hours," Frazier answered.

He didn't translate into civilian time, but Raine figured the jury was starting to get it. "Okay, and how did it come to pass that Mr. Wilson was found dead at five twenty in the morning?"

"Officer Porter went to check on him," Frazier answered, "and found him nonresponsive."

"So, dead?" Raine tried to translate that.

But Frazier wouldn't have it. "Nonresponsive," he

STEPHEN PENNER

repeated. "Only the medical examiner can declare someone dead."

Raine could think of several examples of where a medical examiner would not be needed to declare someone was dead. Officer Porter's death came immediately to mind. But that wasn't the fight.

"What sort of cell was Mr. Wilson in?" Raine asked.

"A jail cell," Frazier sneered.

Raine smiled slightly and nodded. "Thank you, Officer Frazier. I'll ask it a different way. Was he housed with other inmates or in solitary confinement?"

"He was in a solitary confinement cell."

"Was he in there the entire time from booking to being found 'nonresponsive'?" Raine asked.

"Yes," Frazier confirmed. "That's why we had to check on him. We couldn't see him in a common room like we would have with other inmates."

"So what did you do when you opened the door and he was lying on the cell floor not moving?"

"We called for our medical team," Frazier answered.

"Did you call, or did Officer Porter?" Raine asked.

"Does it matter?" Frazier pushed back.

"Let's pretend it might," Raine said. "Who called, you or Porter?"

Frazier took a moment, then answered, "Officer Porter did. I stayed with the body."

"Body? I thought he wasn't dead yet?" Raine needled him.

Frazier didn't respond, but his face got redder.

"Don't worry"—Raine waved a hand at him—"it's a distinction without a difference. Was your medical team able to revive him?"

"No," Frazier growled again.

"So who did you call next?"

"The medical examiner's office," Frazier answered.

"For what purpose?"

"To officially declare him dead," Frazier explained, "and to collect the body."

"At any point between the time you first saw him nonresponsive at five twenty and the time his body was taken away by the staff from the medical examiner's office"—Raine set up the question—"did you see any signs of life whatsoever from Mr. Wilson's body?"

"What kind of signs of life?"

"Anything." Raine threw his hands up. "Movement. Breathing. Opening his eyes. You didn't see anything like that, did you?"

"I did not," Frazier agreed.

"So he was dead at five twenty and probably well before that, wasn't he?" Raine pressed.

But Frazier wouldn't budge. "He was dead when the medical examiner's staff called the on-call medical examiner and he declared him dead."

Raine nodded. "Okay. I guess I'll have to ask them."

"Yeah, do that," Frazier sneered.

"No further questions, Your Honor," Raine announced.

"Any cross-examination, Mr. Pierce?" the judge asked him.

"Yes, Your Honor." Pierce came out from behind his counsel table and approached the witness. "Why was Mr. Wilson placed into solitary confinement?"

"The arresting officer reported he was combative," Frazier answered.

"Thank you," Pierce responded. "No other questions."

Raine stood up, a signal to Buxton-Greene that he wanted to conduct redirect-exam. The judge asked, and he answered in the affirmative.

"Did the arresting officer report that to you personally or a different officer?"

"A different officer."

"Who?"

"Officer Porter."

Raine knew he was going to have to ask eventually. "And where is Officer Porter now?"

Frazier's eyes flashed. "He's dead." If looks could kill, Raine would have joined Porter.

"A motor vehicle accident, I believe," Raine went ahead and told the jurors himself. "Isn't that correct?"

"I'm not convinced it was an accident," was Frazier's reply.

Raine decided not to give him any chance to elucidate. "No further questions."

"Any recross-examination, Mr. Pierce?" Judge Buxton-Greene asked.

Pierce thought for a moment, but then declined. "No, Your Honor. This witness may be excused."

"I don't like those police officers," Ophelia whispered to Raine as Frazier stepped down from the witness stand. "They didn't help Tommy. They're supposed to help people, but they didn't help him at all."

Raine elected not to get into a discussion about whether the role of police was to help people or to enforce laws and how those two roles didn't always overlap. But he wasn't going to apologize for them either. "That's why we're here. Because they didn't do what they were supposed to do."

Ophelia frowned. "It's so hard to sit here and listen to

what they did to my boy. They could have just called me. I would have taken him to rehab. He didn't need to be arrested. He didn't need to go to jail." Then the real point. "He didn't need to die."

Raine couldn't argue with that. In part, because she was right. In part, because the judge interrupted them.

"Any further witnesses for today, Mr. Raine?" she asked.

Raine looked at the clock to confirm he had sufficiently filled the day with witnesses. 4:07 on a Friday. It had been a full week.

"No, Your Honor," he answered as he stood to address the Court. "I think it best if we adjourn for the day and start fresh Monday morning."

Judge Buxton-Greene looked at the clock as well, then nodded. "All right then. The Court will be adjourned until nine o'clock Monday morning."

She banged her gavel, and the bailiff called out for everyone to stand as she exited the courtroom. They were done for the day.

It had gone about as well as it could have with two law enforcement witnesses. They weren't going to help someone suing the jail, but they answered the questions put to them. It was Raine's job to make sure those questions advanced his case. Still, he hoped it would go more smoothly with the next set of witnesses.

At least until he called Nieuwendyk incompetent to his face.

28

B efore calling the next set of witnesses, there was the matter of scheduling Detective Gillespie's testimony, or rather scheduling the service of the subpoena on him for his testimony.

Raine could have tried subpoenaing Kasaybian to the stand, but Gillespie was the better target. Kasaybian would ignore the subpoena, whereas a police officer wouldn't and really couldn't. The judge would make sure his superiors got him to the courtroom. But more importantly, Raine was not nearly as confident in his ability to trick Kasaybian into saying something inculpatory as he was of doing so with Gillespie.

The element of surprise was diminished somewhat by the requirement that the subpoena actually give Gillespie sufficient notice of his required testimony. But Raine could minimize the amount of time the detective had to try to get out of it and/or come up with a story he would try to sell on the stand. Hopefully he'd be overconfident and think his only testimony was to confirm that Officer Porter was dead.

After the trial concluded for the week on Friday afternoon, Raine and Sommers met to work out the timing of her serving the subpoena on Gillespie.

"The first thing, the most important thing," Raine began, "is that you serve him in a public place, not one-on-one with no one else around."

"Why?" Sommers asked.

"Because no one likes to be served with a subpoena," Raine explained. "Having other people around will mute any negative reaction. The more people, the better. You don't want to be alone with an angry cop."

"An angry, dirty cop," Sommers added.

"Exactly." Raine nodded. "Follow him, but don't be conspicuous."

Sommers glanced down at her expensive outfit and tall heels. "Yoga pants and my hair tucked into a hoodie. Got it."

Raine nodded. "Find out his routine and pick a time and place where you know the maximum number of people will be around."

Sommers raised a thoughtful hand to her chin. "That will probably be a weekday. Downtown somewhere. How much time do I have?"

Raine considered the schedule of the upcoming witnesses. "I'm about to call the witnesses who responded to Tommy's cell. Paramedics first, who confirmed he was dead, then the technicians from the medical examiner's office who collected the body. That will take a full day or more."

"Then who?" Sommers asked.

"Then Nieuwendyk," Raine answered.

"So that's another full day, probably," Sommers guessed. "And then Gillespie?"

"And then Gillespie," Raine confirmed. "Serve him after

I'm done with the paramedics and ME techs, but before I finish with Nieuwendyk."

"The day before he has to appear." Sommers grinned. "I like that. No time to think."

"Exactly." Raine smiled.

"What do I say if he asks what he's being subpoenaed to testify about?" Sommers asked. "He might ask that, right?"

"He might," Raine agreed. He frowned for a moment. "Tell him it's just to confirm how Porter died. Don't tell him the real reason."

"And what is the real reason?" Sommers leaned forward. "How does he fit into all of this exactly?"

"Exactly? I'm not sure," Raine admitted. "We'll find that out when Gillespie takes the stand."

29

"The plaintiff calls Caitlyn Decker to the stand." Raine announced the name of the paramedic who first attended to Tommy in the jail cell.

Decker walked to the front of the courtroom with obvious unease. Her job was to help people in medical crisis, not testify about it. She wore a simple cotton dress shirt and dark pants, with comfortable shoes and her brown hair in a ponytail. Despite the comfortable-looking clothes, she appeared decidedly nervous when she sat on the witness stand after being sworn in.

Raine would try to calm her with his initial questions about herself. He wasn't going to attack her testimony. It helped his case. "Could you please state your name for the record?"

"Caitlyn Decker," she almost stammered.

"How are you employed, Ms. Decker?"

"I'm a certified paramedic," she answered.

"Who is your employer?" Raine continued.

"I work at the King County Correctional Facility," she said. "The jail."

"How long have you worked as a paramedic for the King County Jail?"

"I got my paramedic certification last year," Decker answered. "Before that I was a part-time EMT—emergency medical technician—for about six months. So I guess about a year and a half now."

"Were you on duty the morning of the death of Tommy Wilson?"

Decker frowned, but nodded. "Yes."

"Were you called to render aid to Mr. Wilson at approximately five twenty that morning?" Raine continued.

"Yes," Decker answered. "Well, I was called to the cell. I didn't actually end up rendering any aid to him."

"Why is that?" Raine asked.

"Because he was already dead when I arrived," she explained.

"Are you qualified to make that determination?" Raine decided to follow up on Frazier's insistence on death protocols.

"I was in that case," Decker answered. "He had no pulse, and his body was already getting cold to the touch."

"So there was no chance he was alive when you went into that cell?" Raine just wanted it crystal clear.

"No chance, sir," Decker confirmed.

"So what did you do?"

"We backed out of the cell and told the guards to call the ME—the medical examiner."

"Did you wait on scene until the folks from the medical examiner's office arrived?" Raine asked.

"Yes, I did."

"At any point during that time, did anyone do anything to the body?"

Decker shook her head. "No. I was there the whole time. No one else went into the cell until the techs from the ME's office arrived."

"Thank you, Ms. Decker." Raine nodded to her. "No further questions."

Pierce didn't have any questions for Decker either except to confirm that, Tommy being dead when she arrived, she wasn't there to see how he died. Decker agreed with that, and Pierce sat down again.

Raine leaned over to his client while Pierce conducted his sparse questioning. "I know it's hard to have to hear these details," he whispered. "How are you holding up?"

Ophelia offered a weak smile. "I'm okay, Mr. Raine. Thank you for asking. It's not hard to listen to what happened. That's all I ever wanted to know. What's hard is hearing everyone talk about my boy like he's just another drug addict, just another criminal. Like his life didn't matter."

"Of course his life mattered," Raine replied.

"Tell him that." Ophelia pointed at Pierce.

But Raine shook his head and pointed at the jurors. "No. We tell them that."

"Any further questions for this witness, Mr. Raine?" Judge Buxton-Greene interrupted.

Raine stood up. "No, Your Honor."

"Do you have any more witnesses?" the judge asked.

"Oh, yes, Your Honor," was Raine's reply.

RAINE FILLED some time with the other jail medical personnel who were dispatched with Decker and just confirmed none of them even went into the cell. Then he moved on to the medical examiner's office.

"The plaintiff calls Katrina Bergmann to the stand," he announced.

Bergmann was an older woman with strong arms and gray hair pulled into a tight bun at the base of her neck. She showed no signs of nervousness as she strode into the courtroom and approached the judge. She raised a sinewy right hand and swore to tell the truth, the whole truth, and nothing but the truth, then sat on the witness stand and looked at Raine like she was daring him to stop her from doing so.

"Please state your name for the record," Raine began like he always did.

"Katrina Bergmann." There was a slight European accent.

"How are you employed, Ms. Bergmann?"

"I am a scene technician with the King County Medical Examiner's Office." Her accent was rather pleasant, swimming just under the words. Raine guessed it was German, based on her name, but he didn't really know.

Raine gestured to the jury box. "Could you please explain to the jury what a scene technician with the medical examiner's office does?"

Bergmann didn't hesitate to turn to the jurors. "We collect the bodies."

"And what does that entail?" Raine prompted for more information.

Bergmann nodded. "Ah, yes. Well, first we document the body and the location by taking photographs. Then we contact the on-call medical examiner and have them declare the time of death. Then we prepare—"

"Let me interrupt you right there," Raine interjected. "Could you explain a little bit more about how you call the medical examiner to declare the time of death? Is that done over the phone? The doctor doesn't come to the scene?"

Bergmann shook her head. "It is usually not necessary for the doctor to come to the scene. We are trained to know when a person is dead, but only the medical examiner can declare a person dead under the law. So we call the doctor, tell them what we have observed, and then based on that, the doctor makes the call."

"And that's what happened here?" Raine asked. "Was it Dr. Nieuwendyk who made the call as to time of death?"

Bergmann nodded. "Yes, he was on call that night."

"Does the on-call medical examiner also do the autopsy?" Raine asked. He thought the jury might have a similar question.

"I think so," Bergmann tried to answer.

"So the doctor who was up all night on call," Raine reworded Bergmann's answers, "is also supposed to conduct all of the autopsies in the morning?"

"I'm not really involved in who does the autopsies," Bergmann demurred. "I just collect the bodies, you know?"

"Would you agree with me," Raine wasn't going to let her off the hook so easily, "that a person who's been up all night probably shouldn't be making important medical decisions the next day?"

Bergmann shook her head. "I really don't know, sir. I'm not a doctor."

"Well, let me ask it a different way," Raine allowed.

"Would you make an important decision—a life-or-death decision—if you had been awake all night the night before?"

"Would I?" Bergmann stalled.

"Yes," Raine insisted.

Bergmann hesitated, but then admitted, "No, I probably wouldn't. I'm worthless if I don't get enough sleep."

Raine smiled. He liked where they had reached. He knew he was unlikely to convince the jury that Dr. Nieuwendyk was wholly unqualified to conduct an autopsy, but anyone who had almost nodded off while driving knew that sometimes you could be just too tired to do a good job. That insinuation would allow the jurors to find Nieuwendyk incompetent as to Tommy's autopsy specifically, even if he was qualified generally. "No further questions."

Pierce had some questions this time, so after the judge invited him to conduct cross-examination, he stepped out from behind his table and walked toward the witness stand. "Dr. Nieuwendyk is more than qualified to conduct an autopsy, isn't that right?" he started.

"Oh yes," Bergmann answered.

"And he knows how to manage his own schedule, doesn't he?" Pierce continued.

"I'm sure he does," Bergmann agreed.

"So if he felt capable of performing an autopsy toward the end of a graveyard shift," Pierce put to her, "there's no reason to believe he would have been impacted by working a normal eight-hour shift that happened to include a portion of the early hours of the morning. Would you agree with that?"

"I would." Bergmann seemed more than happy to do so. "Yes, sir."

"Good," Pierce replied. "And so the jury is absolutely

clear, you're not suggesting in any way that Dr. Nieuwendyk was incapable of performing the autopsy of Thomas Wilson, are you?"

Raine certainly was. But not Bergmann.

"Oh, no, of course not," she assured him.

Pierce nodded at her. "Okay. Good. I just didn't want there to be any confusion about that. No further questions."

"Any redirect-examination, Mr. Raine?" Judge Buxton-Greene asked.

"No, Your Honor," Raine answered. He was done insinuating Nieuwendyk was incompetent. He was ready to say it to his face. But it would have to wait until after lunch.

"We will adjourn now for the lunch hour," Judge Buxton-Greene announced. It was twelve minutes before noon. Not nearly enough time to call another witness. They would reconvene at 1:00 p.m. sharp.

That was fine with Raine. It would give him a chance to check in with Sommers and make sure the trap was ready to spring.

30

"Did you serve the subpoena on Gillespie?" Raine asked when they were safely inside his office. They didn't dare have their conversation out in a restaurant where someone might overhear it. Laura ordered sandwiches from the joint up the street. There was soda in the fridge. "Did he give you any trouble?"

"Yes and no," Sommers was happy to report.

"Really?" Raine was a bit surprised. "He didn't get upset at all when you handed him the subpoena?"

"He looked annoyed," Sommers said, "but I would be too if someone handed me a subpoena over my lunch hour." She glanced at their lunches on the conference table and laughed. "No subpoenas for us, right?"

"I assume not," Raine answered, "but no promises. Did he say anything at all?"

"He looked at it for a second," Sommers recounted, "then nodded and asked, 'This is that kid who died at the jail, right? You just need me to confirm Porter is dead or something?' I thought that sounded pretty innocuous, so I said, 'Sure.'"

"'Sure'?" Raine questioned. "That's not very certain."

"I was playing the part of a process server, Dan," Sommers protested. "A process server wouldn't know the details of the case, now would she? I'm just doing my job, sir."

Raine laughed. "Okay, fine. I'm glad he doesn't expect what I'm really going to do."

"And what is that exactly?" Sommers asked. "You haven't told me yet."

Raine nodded and took a bite of his sandwich. He washed it down with his drink and pointed his finger at his sometimes investigator. "Step one, I put Nieuwendyk on the stand. I take him through the autopsy and his conclusion, which was that he couldn't reach a conclusion. I'm going to beat him up over that a little bit, but mostly for fun. I don't need to completely discredit him. In fact, I don't want to."

"Why not?" Sommers asked. "Wouldn't that show negligence or something?"

"It would show negligence in the autopsy," Raine answered, "but that happened after the death. I need to show negligence before the death. But even better than negligence is intent."

"Intent?" Sommers lowered her can of soda and squinted at Raine. "You're going to accuse him of intentionally botching the autopsy?"

Raine shook his head. "No, not intent about the autopsy. Intent about the murder."

"Murder?" Sommers set the can of soda down. "You think it was murder?"

Raine nodded. "I do now. And you served a subpoena on the murderer yesterday."

"Detective Gillespie?" Her jaw dropped open. "Why? How? And how are you possibly going to prove it?"

"Think about it." Raine pointed that professorial finger again. "Gillespie is a narcotics detective. What does that mean? It means he runs confidential informants like Tommy. It means he knows drug dealers with lots of money. It means he has a shitty salary and a pension that won't nearly pay West Coast rent prices. It means he knows a lot about drugs. He knows which drugs can cause an overdose. It means he knows which drugs get tested for by the medical examiner's office and which ones don't. And it means he has unquestioned access to the jail. Motive, means, opportunity."

"I'm sorry, what's the motive?" Sommers asked. "Did I miss that? Is it just money or what?"

Raine nodded. "Well, I admit it's a bit of guesswork until he gets on the stand, and I drag it out of him, but it's educated guesswork. He's a government hack who spends his days trying and failing to bring down rich drug dealers like Armand Kasaybian."

"You think Axis Global is a front for a drug import operation?" Sommers feigned surprise. "Ha. Yeah, I knew that the first day we went there."

"I kind of did too," Raine agreed. "They didn't even have any wicker baskets or weird candy anywhere. That's not a real import-export business."

"Have you ever had those British wine gummy candies?" Sommers cringed. "They taste like a grape gave birth to wax."

Raine didn't disagree. "I figure he was running Tommy as an informant, but then Tommy accidentally did a buy from

Axis. Gillespie couldn't follow up on it because he was on the payroll. Tommy realizes what's going on, and Gillespie knows he knows."

"And Tommy was going to turn him in," Sommers interjected.

But Raine shook his head. "I don't think so. He was a drug addict, not a snitch. I doubt he cared about the integrity of the law enforcement system. But he was definitely going to get arrested again for something, and when he did, he'd have that information about Gillespie as a bargaining chip."

Sommers pointed at Raine. "A get-out-of-jail-free card."

"Exactly," Raine confirmed. "Gillespie can't keep him alive, so he waits until he sees Tommy using one night, then calls in an anonymous tip and gets him arrested. Once he's booked, Gillespie shows up at the jail and slips some of that Axis Global money to Porter, who, as we saw from his new car and fancy apartment, was more than willing to be bought off."

"Porter was probably already on the payroll," Sommers added. "Good to have a person inside the jail, and he was living in that fancy apartment."

"Right," Raine agreed. "So all Gillespie has to do is tell Porter to put Tommy in solitary, make up some bullshit reason for it, and let him take care of the rest. Tommy thinks Gillespie is there to get him out, but instead he injects Tommy with some new exotic drug imported by Axis Global from God knows where. Something the medical examiner wouldn't even think to test for. Nieuwendyk said in his deposition that they only get toxicology results for the drugs they ask for. Tommy dies of an overdose, but the tox result comes back clean of the drug, so it's declared natural causes. If Ophelia hadn't made so much noise outside the jail, that probably would have been the end of it."

"That's probably why they went after her so hard," Sommers suggested. "Maybe Porter was even one of the corrections officers who confronted Ophelia outside the jail when she was arrested."

"Maybe," Raine agreed. "In a way, Porter is the key to this. Because you know what narcotics detectives don't do? They don't come to the scene of traffic accident deaths. Unless it's to confirm that the one witness who could identify you as the murderer was also dead."

Raine took another swig of his drink. "I bet that was Gillespie at the pier the night I got arrested. Only an underpaid government employee would drive a beat-up old American sedan. He's probably the one who spotted me."

Sommers took a bite of her sandwich and chewed thoughtfully. "And you're going to get Gillespie to admit all of that on the stand?"

Raine grinned. "Maybe not all of it, but enough of it. If he's smart, he invokes the Fifth Amendment. Everyone will know that means he's guilty. Tommy's murderer is arrested, and Ophelia gets a huge payday."

"As do you." Sommers pointed back at Raine with a big smile. Even with extra arugula on her sandwich, she didn't have any food stuck in her pearly teeth.

"As do I," Raine agreed. "I hope."

"And this all happens after lunch?" Sommers pulled out her phone and swiped her finger across the screen. "I'll have to move a couple of showings, but I'm not going to miss this."

Raine was glad. It was nice to have support. It was even better to have an audience.

"But Nieuwendyk is first," he explained. "He'll tell the

jury all about what drugs they test for and why. Gillespie will be sitting in the hallway, waiting for his turn to testify. As soon as I'm done with Nieuwendyk, you bring Gillespie in, and we wrap up this case once and for all."

Sommers raised her soda can. "Here's to that!"

Raine clinked his can to hers. "What could go wrong?"

31

"The plaintiff calls Dr. Peter Nieuwendyk to the stand," Raine announced after the lunch break.

Everyone was reassembled in the courtroom and fighting off the post-lunch drowsiness that had the danger to suck the energy out of a trial, no matter how compelling the witness. Raine knew he needed to keep his voice elevated and animated. He had made sure his soda was caffeinated.

Nieuwendyk was dressed in a very nice suit, nicer than Raine's, with a crisp white shirt and red silk tie. His shoes were working shoes though. The black sneakers worn by health care professionals who spent all day on their feet. Raine wondered whether there might not be some dried blood on the soles. He decided not to ask.

Instead, he posed his standard first question for every witness. "Please state your name for the record."

"Peter Nieuwendyk," he turned and told the jury. He had obviously testified before. Probably hundreds of times. Part of the job.

"How are you employed, sir?" Raine asked the next question in the introductory series.

"I am an assistant medical examiner with the King County Medical Examiner's Office."

"How long have you been a medical examiner with the King County Medical Examiner's Office?"

It was the same information from the deposition. Work experience. Residencies. Medical school. Too many autopsies to count. There was no doubt Nieuwendyk was qualified to perform an autopsy. He was a career government servant, having eschewed the riches of private practice to use his talents for the greater good.

"Did you conduct the autopsy of Thomas Wilson?" Raine moved on to the case at hand.

"I did," Nieuwendyk confirmed to the jury with a nod.

"Now, before we get to your conclusions," Raine said, "or lack thereof, I'd like to spend a moment to educate the jury a little bit about the possible results of an autopsy."

Nieuwendyk frowned at the "or lack thereof" comment, but he let it go. "Okay."

"Is it fair to say that when conducting an autopsy, you are trying to determine both what we call the cause of death and also the manner of death?" Raine asked, showing off a little of his knowledge to the jurors.

"That is correct," Nieuwendyk agreed.

"Could you explain to the jury the difference between cause of death and manner of death?"

Nieuwendyk turned his entire body in the witness chair to face the jury box fully. "Cause of death refers to the specific mechanism that resulted in death. For example, a gunshot wound to the heart, or sharp force trauma that lacerated an artery, or a drug overdose."

Raine smiled slightly at his inclusion of the actual cause of Tommy Wilson's death, even if he wouldn't be the witness to admit to it.

"And what is manner of death?" Raine prompted.

"Manner of death is a broader category of the type of death it was," Nieuwendyk answered. "Generally speaking, there are four possible manners of death: homicide, suicide, accident, and natural causes. A cause of death could fit into more than one of these categories. Take, for example, a gunshot wound. If someone else shot the person, that would be homicide. If the person shot themselves, that would be suicide. If a gun went off unintentionally and killed the person, that would be accident." He paused. "I'm afraid I can't think of a situation where a gunshot would be natural causes."

There were a couple of light laughs from the jury box at Nieuwendyk's last comment.

"How do you determine the cause of death and the manner of death?" Raine continued.

"That's what the autopsy is for," Nieuwendyk answered. "The purpose of an autopsy is to examine the body and draw conclusions from what you observe on the body."

"Do you also consider outside information?" Raine asked. "If you're trying to decide between homicide and suicide, do you care if a suicide note was left behind?"

Nieuwendyk frowned. "No. I never read the police reports before I conduct an autopsy."

"Why is that?" Raine inquired.

"Outside information can prejudice my analysis," Nieuwendyk explained, "and I don't want what the police think happened to cloud my judgment of what I think happened."

"How would police reports cloud your judgment?" Raine followed up.

"Let's take a gunshot wound to the head as an example." Nieuwendyk turned again to the jurors. "And let's say the police found a suicide note at the scene. Well, a suicide note might be genuine, or it might be forged by a murderer."

"Good point," Raine allowed.

"I'm not a detective," Nieuwendyk continued. "The detective will gather all of the relevant evidence and make a determination about the veracity of the note. My autopsy might be one of those pieces of evidence that impacts the appraisal of that suicide note. It shouldn't be the other way around."

"What do you mean?" Raine asked.

"As a forensic pathologist," Nieuwendyk answered, "I know that gunshot wounds from suicide usually look different than gunshot wounds from homicide. A person who killed themselves will usually press the barrel against the flesh, leaving what we call a sealed gunshot wound. There will be notable burning and stippling inside the wound from the unexploded gunpowder particles that follow the bullet out of the barrel. A person who is shot by another person will usually flinch away from the barrel, resulting in perhaps a contact wound, but not a sealed wound, and a lot of that burning and stippling will be on the surface of the skin outside of the wound. I don't want to read the police report to know there was a suicide note. I want to tell the detective whether it was suicide or not so they know whether the suicide note is legitimate."

Raine liked that answer. The jury did too. He was relieved he wasn't going to have to try to make Nieuwendyk out as incompetent after all. He wasn't sure he would have succeeded.

"What about drug overdoses?" Raine asked. "How do you determine that? Drugs don't leave behind gunpowder burns, right?"

"Right," Nieuwendyk agreed. "While in some cases there might be visible pathologies to certain organs, it is generally not going to be possible to conclude a death was a drug overdose without toxicology results. You never would anyway. You need the toxicology results to be sure."

"How are toxicology results obtained?" Raine continued the examination. "Do you do them yourself?"

"No," Nieuwendyk answered. "We collect blood samples from the body and send those to the Washington State Toxicology Laboratory. The scientists there test the blood for controlled substances and then send us a written report."

"What substances do they test for?" Raine asked.

"In the case of a suspected overdose," Nieuwendyk explained to the jury, "there are standard drugs they will always test for. Cocaine, heroin, methamphetamine, opioids. Not cannabis though. There are no documented cases of anyone ever dying from an overdose of cannabis. Anything else, you would have to specifically request."

Raine supposed that was interesting, if not directly relevant to Tommy's case.

"Okay, so let's talk about your autopsy of Thomas Wilson," Raine directed. "Were you able to determine a cause of death or a manner of death?"

"I was able to determine a manner of death," Nieuwendyk answered, "but I was not able to determine a cause of death."

"Let's start with the cause of death," Raine instructed. "Why weren't you able to determine one?"

"Because there was no obvious trauma to the body,"

Nieuwendyk explained to the jurors. "There were no gunshot wounds or sharp force or blunt force trauma injuries. Basically, his body did not bear any signs of a mechanism that would have caused his death."

"So if you were unable to determine a cause of death," Raine challenged, "how could you determine a manner of death?"

"In large part, it was the fact that there was no obvious cause of death that led to my conclusion as to manner of death," the doctor answered. "I was able to rule out homicide, suicide, and accident. That left natural causes, and that was my determination."

"What about a drug overdose?" Raine asked. "You just testified that often drug overdoses don't have any obvious signs of injury."

"Even though he was arrested for drug possession, I was able to rule out a drug overdose based on the toxicology results," Nieuwendyk answered. "There were low levels of opiates and amphetamine, but nothing close to a level that could kill a person."

Something about that answer hit Raine wrong, but he was eager to ask the next question. The big question. The one that would set up his unmasking of Detective Gillespie.

"Is it possible Mr. Wilson could have overdosed on a drug that the Toxicology Laboratory didn't test for?" he suggested. "Perhaps some new drug that had just hit the streets?"

"Uh..." Nieuwendyk hesitated. "Is it possible? I suppose anything is possible, but—"

"How does the Tox Lab know what substances to test for?"

"As I said, there are a series of common drugs they

always test for," Nieuwendyk answered. "I can also indicate any additional drugs I want them to test for."

"Why would you do that?"

Nieuwendyk shrugged. "If I wanted them to find it, I imagine."

Raine formulated the next obvious question in his mind, the corollary to Nieuwendyk's answer. But the question stuck in his throat when he realized what it meant.

He took a moment. Then another. The entire courtroom was waiting on him.

"Mr. Raine?" Judge Buxton-Greene called down. "Do you have any further questions for this witness?"

Raine took another beat, then shook his head. But he didn't say no. He said, "I need a recess, Your Honor. I would move to adjourn for the day."

"Adjourn?" the judge scoffed. She looked at the clock on the wall. "We still have almost the entire afternoon."

"I'm sorry, Your Honor," Raine apologized, "but I just remembered something. That is, something just came up. I mean, I have to leave now. I can't ask any more questions right now, but I'm not done with my examination. I need a recess. I need to adjourn for the day."

Pierce stood up to address the Court. "I would object, Your Honor. If Mr. Raine is finished with the doctor, then I should be allowed to cross-examine him now."

"I'm not finished with him," Raine protested. "I'm just finished for today."

Judge Buxton-Greene stared down at Raine. "Are you okay, Mr. Raine?"

That might be the angle, Raine decided. "No, Your Honor. I'm not. I'd rather not be required to provide a fuller explanation, especially not on the record and in front of the jury." He placed a hand over his gut to suggest, but technically not actually say, that he might be suffering from a stomach ailment that could end up being unpleasant for everyone assembled.

Buxton-Greene frowned at him, but didn't say no.

"Your Honor," Pierce complained, "this is highly irregular. I believe Mr. Raine even has another witness waiting in the hallway. Clearly, he planned to be in session all afternoon."

"Plans change, Mr. Pierce," the judge answered. She looked again at Raine. "Mr. Raine, are you telling me, as an officer of the Court, that you need to adjourn for the remainder of the day?"

Raine nodded. "That is exactly what I am telling you, Your Honor, yes."

Buxton-Greene sighed audibly, but then nodded and addressed the jurors. "You have my apologies, ladies and gentlemen, but we are going to have to adjourn for the day. Do not concern yourselves with the reasons why. We will reconvene tomorrow morning at nine a.m. sharp." Another glance at Raine. "And, Mr. Raine?"

"Yes, Your Honor."

"No further delays," she informed him. "You will finish your questioning, or you will rest your case. Is that understood?"

"Perfectly, Your Honor," Raine answered. "Thank you, Your Honor."

Buxton-Greene frowned at the repeated "Your Honors," but she'd given him what he wanted.

He waited for her to stand up to leave, then went directly to Sommers. "Meet me in my office in exactly one hour."

"What's going on?" Sommers asked.

"I'll explain it then," Raine promised. "We have a busy night ahead of us."

Sommers agreed and departed the courtroom. Raine returned to his client.

"What's going on, Mr. Raine?" Ophelia asked.

Raine glanced around the still too-crowded courtroom. The judge and the jurors had left, but the court staff and Pierce were still there, and Nieuwendyk was still seated on the witness stand, looking very confused.

"I can't explain right now," he offered. "I just need you to trust me."

"Of course I trust you," Ophelia responded.

Raine was heartened to hear that.

"What do you need me to do?" Ophelia asked.

Raine considered for a moment. "I need you to go home, get a good night's rest, and meet me back here tomorrow morning."

"That's it?" she asked.

"That's it," Raine confirmed with a smile. "I'll take care of the rest."

Ophelia smiled back. She shook Raine's hand, thanked him, and headed for the exit as well.

"I think you're losing it, Raine," Pierce called out to him from his counsel table. "I'm looking forward to seeing if you can pull it together by tomorrow."

Raine was too.

He waited for Pierce to leave, then hurried over to Nieuwendyk. They were the only two left in the courtroom.

"I'm sorry to have interrupted your testimony, Dr. Nieuwendyk," Raine offered, his face as serious as he could muster. "I need to talk to you about Detective Leo Gillespie and how he was involved in Tommy Wilson's murder."

"Murder?" Nieuwendyk gasped.

"Can you meet me tonight?" Raine asked, glancing around the empty courtroom.

"Um, yes," Nieuwendyk agreed. "Yes. When? Where?"

"Seven p.m. Pier 32 on the south waterfront," Raine answered. "There's something I want to show you. Do you know where that is?"

"I'm sure I can find it," Nieuwendyk answered. "Seven p.m., you said?"

"Yes," Raine confirmed. "And, Doctor?"

"Yes?"

Raine looked around the courtroom again, then locked eyes with Nieuwendyk. "Come alone."

32

Raine was already at the entrance to Pier 32 when Nieuwendyk arrived. The doctor parked his Ford Taurus directly across from the pier and crossed the street quickly before carefully stepping over the large puddle that stretched half the length of the joint between the wood of the pier and the asphalt of the road. The rain that had let up earlier in the afternoon was trying to return. Ringlet waves appeared in the puddle, lit by the lampposts of the pier.

"What did you want to show me, Mr. Raine?" Nieuwendyk asked. "And what does Detective Gillespie have to do with all of this?"

Raine gestured for Nieuwendyk to follow him farther out on the pier. They approached the building for Axis Global, but Raine stopped them before they quite reached the structure. He pointed at the building.

"This is supposedly the headquarters of a business called Axis Global Import-Export," Raine told him, "but it's actually a front for an international drug operation run by a man named Armand Kasaybian."

"Okay," Nieuwendyk replied. "What does this have to do with Detective Gillespie? Or me, for that matter?"

Raine nodded. The rain was starting to prick at his face. "It took a while, but I finally put two and two together. Tommy Wilson was running drug deliveries for Axis Global. But he was also working as a confidential informant for Detective Gillespie. But Gillespie was on Axis Global's payroll. He was on the take, looking the other way as whatever cartel is behind this sham business started flooding our streets with the latest deadly drug. Tommy accidentally found out Gillespie was working for Axis Global, so Gillespie had to get rid of him. He couldn't leave an unreliable drug addict alive with that kind of information. So he arranged for Tommy to get arrested, then sneaked into the jail with the help of a corrupt guard and injected Tommy with a drug you wouldn't know to test for when you did the autopsy. That's why the tox report was clean."

Nieuwendyk nodded along with Raine's recitation. "Wow," he said after a moment. "That's amazing. I can't believe you figured that out."

"The only thing I need to know is what the drug was," Raine told the doctor. "What's a drug that you wouldn't test for but that could make someone have an overdose a few hours after taking it?"

"A few hours later?" Nieuwendyk questioned. "Oh, I mean. Not many. Most drugs have fairly immediate effects. That's why people take them."

"Of course, of course," Raine agreed. "But if you needed it to be delayed, how would you do that?"

"Uh, I guess with a coated pill," Nieuwendyk answered.

"Like a deadly dose of ketamine but in a hard-to-digest capsule?" Raine asked.

"Something like that," Nieuwendyk confirmed after a moment. Then he frowned. "But if Gillespie could sneak into and out of the jail, why would he need a time-delayed capsule?"

"He wouldn't," Raine answered. "But you would, so by the time the ketamine killed him, he'd be inside the jail, and it would look like natural causes instead of a drug overdose."

What color was visible in Nieuwendyk's face in the dim light drained away.

"At first I thought it was probably fentanyl," Raine continued, "but that's an opioid, and you couldn't ask the Tox Lab not to test for opioids. That would have raised questions. But ketamine is a pharmaceutical, an anesthetic. You said they would only test for that if you asked. So you track him down and give him the pill on a night you know you'll be on call. That makes sure you'll be the one who does the autopsy. Then you have him arrested and make sure Porter puts him in solitary so no one will help him. He dies of a ketamine overdose, but no one can prove it because you don't order a test for ketamine. The tox result comes back clean of anything that could have killed him. So natural causes and case closed."

Nieuwendyk stared a hole through Raine but didn't say anything. Which meant he didn't deny it.

"After all, who's going to miss another dead drug addict?" Raine concluded. Then he clapped his hands and pointed at Nieuwendyk. "Oh! His mom, as it turns out."

Nieuwendyk took a step back. "Why would I do any of that?"

"Pretty much the same reasons I thought Gillespie did

it." Raine pointed to Nieuwendyk's car. "How old is that anyway? Didn't Ford stop making the Taurus years ago? How much debt do you have from medical school? You can't be making that much as a government employee. What are your friends from medical school making now? I heard anesthesiologists make the most. Is that true? How much more do they make than you?"

Raine gestured at the Axis Global building.

"But the most important question is, how did you get wrapped up in all this?" Raine asked. "Did you answer an ad, or were they looking for someone with scientific knowledge of drugs? I mean, you're an excellent choice except for the fact that you keep coming here and being seen by people. I saw your car the night I was roughed up here. I'm guessing Tommy saw you here too. Probably overheard a conversation between you and Kasaybian. Heard your name. Maybe your job title. No, you can't leave someone like that alive. That's a loose end. If you're going to play this game, you can't have any loose ends."

Nieuwendyk stared at Raine for several seconds; then he shook his head and laughed. "You couldn't just sue the county for Mommy and move on to your next case, could you? You just had to try to solve some puzzle you thought you saw, because lawyers see conspiracies everywhere. And now here you are, you stupid lawyer, but you know what else you are? You're a loose end too." He reached around and pulled a handgun out of the back of his waistband. "And you're right. I can't have any loose ends."

Nieuwendyk leveled the handgun at Raine's chest.

Raine raised his hands and started backing up toward the warehouse. "You don't want to do this, Doctor," he said. "You don't want to commit two murders."

"I'm pretty sure if I get caught for one, I'll get the same sentence if I do two," Nieuwendyk replied.

Raine lowered his hands slightly. "You'd think so, but actually no. Even first-degree murder, you could get only twenty years—twenty-five if you use a gun. But a second murder is going to run consecutive by statute, so then it's functionally a life sentence."

"Shut up, Raine," Nieuwendyk growled. "I'm not going to prison for any of this. I know how to make a drug overdose look like natural causes, and I know how to make a shooting death look like self-defense. I don't suppose you'd be willing to lean forward and run at me so the bullet trajectories are more consistent with my story?"

"No," Raine answered. "But by the way, that's how I figured it out."

"Figured what out?" Nieuwendyk scowled at him.

"That it was you." Raine was still taking small steps backward, hands raised. Nieuwendyk was still taking larger steps toward him. "You testified near the beginning of your testimony that you never read the police reports, but then you said Tommy was arrested for drug possession. You wouldn't have known that without reading the reports unless you were the one who called the cops."

"Bravo," Nieuwendyk sneered. "One last puzzle solved by the righteous lawyer. I hope you enjoyed that last victory. Goodbye, Mr. Raine."

Nieuwendyk pulled the trigger. Two shots, center mass.

33

Raine's body flew backward from the force of the bullets, and he landed face up directly in front of the door to Axis Global Import-Export. The rain pelted his motionless body.

A moment later the door to the business opened, and out stepped Detective Leo Gillespie, his own firearm raised and pointed directly at Nieuwendyk. "Peter Nieuwendyk, you are under arrest for the murder of Thomas Wilson."

In case Nieuwendyk had any thoughts about trying his luck in a shoot-out, two uniformed officers with rifles came around the far corner of the warehouse, their weapons also aimed at Nieuwendyk's chest. Behind them was Rebecca Sommers, who rushed over and knelt beside Raine. Nieuwendyk looked over his shoulder, but there were two more officers stepping onto the pier to close off that avenue of escape.

Nieuwendyk hesitated for a moment, then dropped his handgun onto the wood and raised his hands in surrender. "At least I took that lawyer out first."

Raine groaned and sat up, grasping at his chest. "I feel like I got punched by two rhinos."

"The vest is bulletproof"—Gillespie laughed—"but your chest isn't bruise-proof. You're going to hurt for a few days, Raine."

A small price to pay to bring justice to a grieving mother.

"NICE WORK, YOU TWO." Detective Gillespie came over to where Raine and Sommers were seated on the curb of the pier. "I'm glad I decided to believe you."

Raine looked up at the detective. His chest still hurt. Those bruises were going to take a long time to heal. "Why did you?"

Sommers smacked him on the arm, the resultant movement causing the bruises to throb. "Because I am very convincing, Dan."

"That's true," Gillespie agreed. "But I did it for Tommy. He had his struggles, but he deserved better than what happened to him."

"So he really was one of your informants?" Raine was gratified he'd deduced that properly.

"Occasionally," Gillespie confirmed. "You do this job long enough to meet a lot of addicts. Some of them get clean. Some of them overdose. Most of them just keep on being addicts. You arrest someone enough times, you start to see them as a person to be helped more than a criminal to be arrested."

"Or an asset to be exploited," Raine pointed out. "If they ever really get clean, they wouldn't be of use to you as an informant."

Gillespie shrugged. "If one of them gets clean, that's great. There's a hundred more who aren't. Of those, there's a handful who are smart enough and trustworthy enough to recruit as an informant. They have the connections, I give them the cash, they buy the drugs, and the bad guy gets arrested. Win-win."

Raine didn't have strong feelings about detectives and informants. But he had developed strong feelings about Tommy. "You should have protected him."

Gillespie sighed. Then he nodded. "You're right. I failed. But I was trying to make up for it."

"How so?" Sommers asked with a tilt of her head.

"You weren't the only one trying to talk to Porter the day he died," Gillespie explained. "I was in the lobby too when he came down, and saw you then took off running." He patted his thick gut and laughed. "I couldn't possibly keep up with you two in a foot chase, so I was just going to come back later. But then the call came in of a pedestrian-vehicle fatality accident just a few blocks away. I took the call because I thought it might be one of you two. I guessed one of you ran into traffic because you weren't watching where you were going. I didn't expect to find out Porter jumped in front of a truck rather than talk to some lawyer. But that's when I knew he was dirty and something bigger was going on."

"And that's why you believed Rebecca when she told you our plan," Raine said.

Sommers smacked him again, sending the bruises throbbing again. "He believed me because I'm convincing."

Gillespie smiled. "Well, it's a good thing for you that I did, Raine. If she hadn't convinced me, you would have met

Tommy's murderer alone, without one of our bulletproof vests under your shirt."

"If she hadn't convinced you," Raine replied, "Nieuwendyk would have found himself alone on this pier, wondering where the hell I was. I'm not an idiot."

Gillespie laughed. "Well, whatever you are, you've got a good partner, Raine. Don't let her get away."

Raine looked at Sommers. Sommers returned a satisfied grin.

"Don't worry," Raine answered. "Like I said, I'm not an idiot."

EPILOGUE

Nieuwendyk was charged with the murder of Tommy Wilson. Kasaybian disappeared before the police could arrest him. And Pierce settled the case immediately upon learning the truth.

"This is for you." Raine slid the check across the conference table to Ophelia Wilson. It took a few days to finalize the exact terms of the settlement, especially the part that followed the dollar sign, and it took a few more days for the money to hit Raine's trust account. But as soon as it did, he had Laura make the appointment and wrote the check himself, holding back a third as his contingency fee, of course.

Ophelia's eyes widened as she picked up the check and held it up to examine it, as if it weren't really happening. "This is a lot of money."

It was. Not life-altering, but enough to make sure Ophelia would live out her days in comfort. Raine might not be able to live in comfort from his share, but it would keep the lights on for a couple of years.

"They needed to pay for what happened," Raine replied.

Ophelia nodded slowly, then set the check down on the table again. When she looked up, her eyes were glistening. "I'll never forget what you did for me, Mr. Raine," she said. "Or for Tommy."

Raine hadn't done anything for Tommy. Tommy was still dead. But at least he didn't die a lonely drug addict. He died a victim of drugs and corruption, with people who cared about him and fought for him after his death.

"Just doing my job," Raine insisted. But they both knew it had become more than that.

He was glad he crossed the street that day.

WE HOPE YOU ENJOYED THIS BOOK

If you could spend a moment to write an honest review on Amazon, no matter how short, we would be extremely grateful. They really do help readers discover new authors.

ALSO BY STEPHEN PENNER

Rain City Legal Thriller Series

Burden of Proof

Trial By Jury

The Survival Rule

Double Jeopardy

Made in the USA
Columbia, SC
04 July 2024

38058490R10155